WHEN DREAMS REMEMBER

WHEN DREAMS REMEMBER

A Novel

Jacqueline Heller

International Psychoanalytic Books (IPBooks)
New York • IPBooks.net

Published by IPBooks, Queens, NY
Online at: www.IPBooks.net

This book is a work of fiction. Names, characters, places, events, and incidents are fictitious. Any resemblance to actual persons, living or dead, or to historical figures is intended purely for literary exploration and not as an exact representation. This novel draws upon historical, psychological, and scientific research, but dramatizes these elements for narrative purposes.

Quoted material or citations provide an educational and literary context. This work honors, but does not replicate, or accurately predict, historical or scientific facts.

ISBN 978-1-969031-09-0

Contents

Author's Note vii

Hannah's Genealogy Tree ix

Chapter 1: The Assignment 1

Chapter 2: The Chest 5

Chapter 3: Letters 11

Chapter 4: Between Us (*Entre Nous*) 17

Chapter 5: Hannah's Diary 25

Chapter 6: The Yellow Diary 1 31

Chapter 7: Yellow Diary 2 39

Chapter 8: Something in the Air 45

Chapter 9: The Interview 51

Chapter 10: Dreams and Genes 59

Chapter 11: Unraveling Threads 73

Chapter 12: Grounded 77

Chapter 13: Storytelling 85

Chapter 14: The Bath 101

Chapter 15: Echoes From Ella 105

Chapter 16: In the Flesh 113

Chapter 17: Lineage and Linkage 121

Chapter 18: Good and Wicked 131

Chapter 19: The Lovers 139

Chapter 20: Countess Madeleine 145

Chapter 21: The Witch Trial 155

Chapter 22: Wise Elders 169

Chapter 23: Have Faith 177

Chapter 24: Family Ties 181

Chapter 25: Succession 187

Glossary of Terms 193

About Jacqueline Heller 197

Acknowledgments 198

Author's Note

This story is about memory, not as neatly recorded, but as lived and reshaped across generations. It is about the invisible forces that shape who we are long before we can speak.

Some wounds leave traces on the body, the mind, the spirit, and in our silence. However, connected by hope, resilience, and belonging, our connections grow, link by link, from the remnants of what we survive, the meaning we make of our lives, and the stories we tell.

Many generations of family records are fragmented or have been lost to war, exile, persecution, migration, erasure, and the silence of trauma left behind. Hannah Glass is descended from two significant and divergent legacies: one rooted in nobility, the other in ancient scholarship. On her maternal grandmother's side, she traced her lineage back to Countess Madeleine du Beaune, a French noblewoman born in 1620. Her line carried through Jacques du Beaune and across centuries of upheaval to Maria Berg. On her paternal grandfather's side, she inherited the name and spiritual heritage of Rabbi Joel Nathan Levi, a 17th-century Talmudic scholar whose son Aaron Levi continued the male line that led to Zachary Levi, who, in union with Maria, brought the two lines full circle.

Hannah is their granddaughter, born of both Torah and title. Here is her story.

Hannah's Genealogy Tree

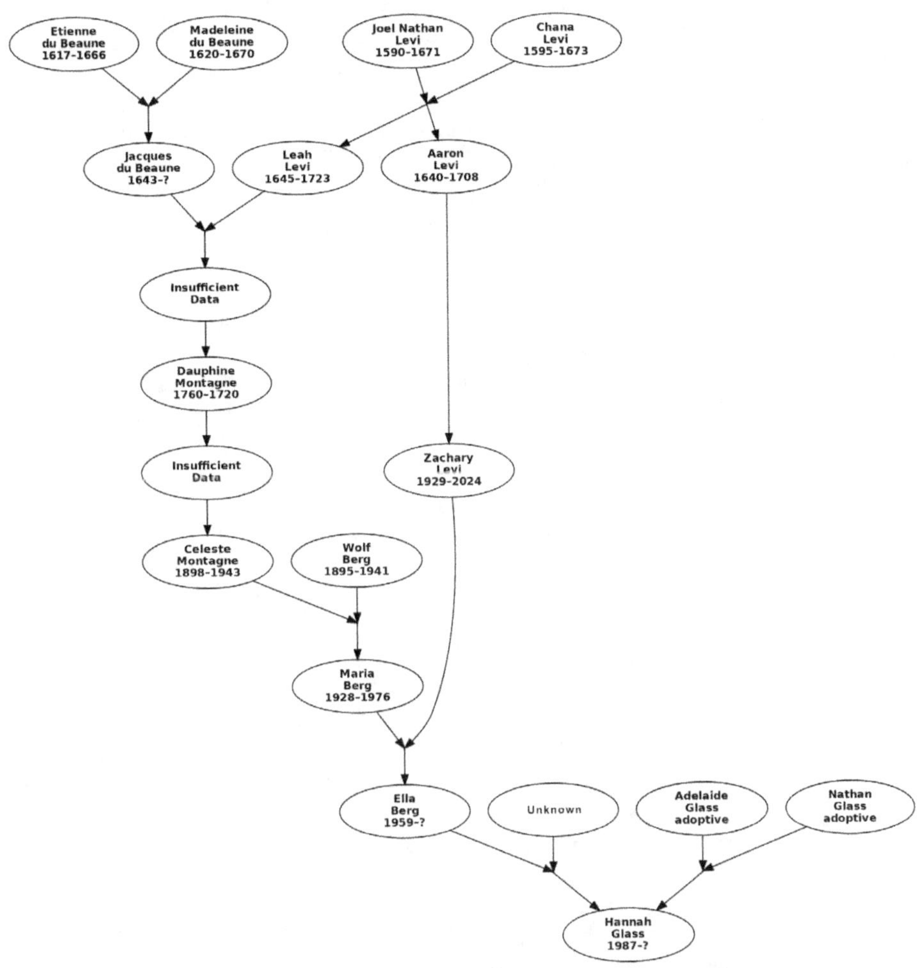

Dedicated to my late parents,

Joseph Heller and Fanya Gottesfeld Heller,

who survived the Holocaust.

Chapter 1: The Assignment

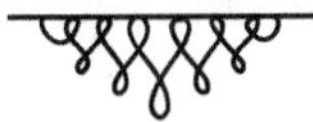

Hannah sat in a small café in Greenwich Village, notebook in hand, trying not to overthink her next big assignment. It was still early morning, and the café was empty except for a couple of freelancers with earbuds and screens. A barista was wiping down the tables. Outside, slush melted in streaks, the remnants of a March storm. Hannah stirred the foam in her cappuccino without taking a sip. She preferred bitter drinks—black coffee and unsweetened tea—but she had recently ordered cappuccinos, as if the foamy milk might blunt or soothe the edginess she felt inside her.

The café started to fill up. The hum of conversation around her was distracting yet comforting, making her feel like part of a community. The rain outside gave the day a cozy intimacy as if the world had tucked itself in just for her. A couple holding hands passed by the window, laughing. Hannah felt the familiar pang of absence.

Sophie, her Type-A Gen X editor, had sent an email that morning: "One for the 'Mind Matters' column. Psychoanalysis is trending again, thanks to TikTok therapists and trauma talk. Do a profile on this, Dr. Jo Brightman. She has a book, clients, controversy, and some edge. See what all the buzz is about—what makes her different."

The editor's voice rang: "Get something no one else can. Get under her skin, Hannah. The piece is due in about 12 weeks, with no hard deadline. I want something real, not fluff."

Hannah stared at the message, and then Googled the name: Dr. Josephine Brightman, a Manhattan psychiatrist and psychoanalyst in her mid-60s, was known for writing about inherited trauma—a term that was new to Hannah. She felt a familiar skepticism. She had a reflexive need to question bold claims, phrases like, "Sometimes wounds aren't even from our lives. They can be handed down, like an heirloom."

Hannah was not sure she believed in inherited trauma. She believed in trauma, but not the kind that tiptoed across generations like some invisible heirloom. And yet, here she was, assigned to interview someone who claimed exactly that.

Hannah had Dr. Brightman's *Yesterday Never Rests* book on her laptop. She scanned the book and found that this inherited trauma concept was edging toward the very heart of Dr. Jo's work. She found a passage that clearly explained that we cannot inherit someone else's trauma. Still, we can be deeply impacted by the emotional effects of trauma that others carry with them, especially in interactions between parents and young children.

She opened her laptop and began drafting a note to the doctor, trying to sound professional but warm. "Dear Dr. Brightman, I'm writing an article for *Currents,* a long-form magazine that explores the inner life." The words felt stiff, so she deleted them.

What was the story she was writing? She wrote in her notebook: "Inherited grief does not knock. It seeps. Slow. Familiar. It sneaks up on you and leaves traces, like perfume you forgot you wore."

Outside, a delivery truck stalled in the intersection. The driver honked, then gave up. Hannah watched a woman in a dark coat help a child across the icy crosswalk, her hand steady on the boy's shoulder. The child reminded her, suddenly, of Elijah.

Hazel, Hannah's aunt, used to call Elijah her miracle. A foster baby with night terrors and darting eyes, he came to live with her aunt when Hannah was 13. Hazel and her mother, Addie, were cut from the same cloth; both believed in *tikkun olam,* a Hebrew term that defines repairing the world with charitable deeds. They both thought love could rescue anyone. Hazel kept Elijah close, singing him Yiddish lullabies and wrapping him in hand-knit sweaters. "We are stitched from the same thread," she told Hannah once, her voice tender and tired. "Even if we forget or don't recognize the pattern."

Hazel died five years later. The agency placed Elijah with another family, and Hannah never saw him again.

Hannah realized that watching this child cross the street reminded her of how David used to rest his warm and grounding hand on her neck when they crossed the street in winter. She had not expected that detail to return, and it hit her like a ton of bricks. David, her fiancé, had crossed the street that day ahead of Hannah, and that was the end of his journey. Hazel, Elijah, and David were here one minute and gone the next. Hannah shivered, realizing she was so lucky. She could have easily taken the place of either Elijah or David.

She reached for her cup, suddenly unsure of what was sadness and what was a memory. And why is this morbid stuff on her brain, she wondered.

She shook the thought away. Grief and tragic loss were not part of the article, or were they?

Dr. Brightman had written about ghosts. "Not the spooky kind," Hannah remembered from the website, "but the kind we carry in our bodies, our silences, our dreams." She clicked open another tab and began reading the first pages of the doctor's book, *Yesterday Never Rests.* The prose was lyrical and precise. Something about it unsettled her.

She read: "We inherit more than eye color and bone structure. We inherit memory, too. The unspoken, unprocessed residue of what came before us."

Hannah closed the book. Wasn't that just a metaphor? Or was it real? She did not know.

She took out her notebook and began jotting down questions:

What do we owe the dead?

Is memory a choice?

Can pain be passed down, cell to cell?

Then she wrote one more:

What if I am not just writing a profile?

Outside, the woman and child were gone. The café was warm, but Hannah's cappuccino was cold. She took a sip, dropped some money on the table, and took off.

Chapter 2: The Chest

At the epic Woodstock Music Festival in New York in 1969, which drew half a million people, Nate and Adelaide met while singing and dancing to Sly and the Family Stone's "I Want to Take You Higher." When the rains came, they huddled together under a sodden blanket and fell in love quickly.

Wearing cutoffs, beads, and long hair, they soon married in a small outdoor ceremony in Tuxedo, New York, while a friend with a guitar played and sang The Beatles' "All You Need Is Love." Adelaide, or "Addie," was only 22 years old.

They were carefree spirits. Nate was a self-proclaimed and talented carpenter. They settled in an old fixer-upper in Cold Spring Harbor on Long Island, and began their new lives with hope for themselves and for humanity.

After years of struggling with infertility and not conceiving children on their own, Nate and Addie decided to adopt. Addie had no idea how difficult it would be to become pregnant, and neither did she realize how difficult it would be to go through the adoption process. But that was how they found Hannah, a beautiful baby with almond-shaped brown eyes, in an orphanage in New York City. Only two months old, she looked at them, chewed on her little fist, and smiled. Nate always said it was her smile that captured his heart.

Hannah grew up well-loved. She made friends easily, and enjoyed a life full of fun, travel, and friendships. But Hannah's anxiety attacks had already begun in her teens, and neither parent could figure out why she was having panic attacks since she had an idyllic childhood.

The terror first took hold when Hannah was only 14 years old, as she witnessed on television the terrorist attack on 9/11 in nearby New York City. Then, she saw David, her fiancé, die as he was struck by a bus in Manhattan when she was a young woman. Only then, in the aftermath of her grief, did she really begin to think about her origins.

The Glasses supposed that panic attacks were emotionally based and not due to physiology or biological inheritance. Over time, they learned from doctors that it was not as simple as nature versus nurture, but was a constant interaction of biological, genetic, physiological, and emotional factors. After much education, Hannah tried Prozac for a few years, which helped. But the side effects became intolerable, so she had to discontinue the medication, and was not inclined to try any others.

When Hannah became a traveling journalist, after five years of directing the Barnard Writing Fellows program, she decided she needed to investigate her past and learn about her birth mother. In part, she wanted to know her genetic history; was there any connection between her panic attacks and genealogy?

Zachary Levi, a long-lost relative in England, found Hannah before she embarked on her quest to find her birth mother. His close advisor, Mr. Graham Pauly, had contacted Hannah several weeks before to inform her of her connection to Zach, that she was his sole heir; and to tell her about a vintage chest being shipped to New York. She approved shipping the chest to her parents' house because her apartment in New York was impossibly small.

⁘

Every Thursday morning, the captain of the mail boat backed into Little Cold Spring Harbor, where he transferred mail and packages to the dock. However, the British freight forwarder arranged to load the crated chest onto the next mail boat to Cold Spring Harbor. Somehow, the crate cracked apart during the journey between the harbor and the mail boat, exposing the wooden chest.

With finagling and a few exasperated groans, two men could finally balance the chest on the boat's old, oxidized dolly. Halfway down the gangplank, the hand wheels on the dolly began to buckle. The cumbersome piece started teetering precariously toward the sea. They continued down the ramp by maneuvering the beleaguered dolly forward, bumping clumsily with each turn of its crippled wheels.

"You need to get to the gym, old man," the younger one, Henry, teased as they set the cumbersome piece down. George, the older one, gave him a look.

"You know what I mean? Work off some of that flab." Henry grinned as he pointed at George's bulging midsection. He then patted his hard six-pack. "See this? It is all muscle! I'm telling you, that belly of yours is why this thing almost got the best of us." Henry gave his stomach several hard hits and smiled. "Now, a ripped body like this here, well, you get the picture, right?"

"Yeah, yeah," George said with a disagreeable shrug. "I'll tell you what, kid, when you're big enough to start shaving, I'll listen. After watching you scarf down six donuts this morning, I guarantee you'll look like me when you're 40. You wait!"

The younger one guffawed, as if such a thing were impossible, and then playfully elbowed his coworker's side. The captain heard their friendly banter as they returned up the ramp.

The captain, who had kept his eyes on them, called out from the front of the craft, "Hoy, mates! Get moving and get this old girl out of here." *What in the heavens could be in that old chest*, the captain wondered as he lifted his cap to cover his eyes from the intense glare of the island sun. He stooped down to grab a couple of cold beers to pitch to his crew members.

Addie had snuck out to do some shopping when the antique chest arrived. She would not have scheduled so many clients that day at her home office if she had known the delivery would be arriving from England. Its arrival was, Addie realized, a momentous occasion that could be life-changing for Hannah. Her heart pounded with excitement.

For years, Hannah was embarrassed by her mother's lack of sophistication and Pollyanna ways. A psychotherapist with a master's degree in Marriage, Family, and Child Counseling (MFCC), earned years earlier, Addie also incorporated astrology and a new-age, crystal-based spiritual practice into her work. Despite her unconventional approach, Addie was kind-hearted, well-liked by clients, and stayed busy.

Nate called Addie's cell to inform her of the arrival and that he had instructed the men to take it upstairs to the attic. "But Nate," she said, "It's so hot, and those stairs can be treacherous." She'd naively thought it would be obvious to him that this precious chest did not belong in a remote location or a non-temperature-controlled room, rather than the living room.

"Honey, we just don't have enough room to store it downstairs," Nate said. Stuff crowded the first two floors of their Victorian house; after all, they had lived there for 33 years and raised Hannah there. The rooms were large and rambling, but everything was already in place, with little space to maneuver pieces of furniture. Their space became exceptionally crowded with both of their offices on the first floor; their city workplaces had been eliminated during the COVID-19 pandemic, and they saw no reason to revert to their previous setup.

"Have them move it to the sunroom for now," Addie instructed. *What a dumb idea to drag anything heavy up to the third floor!* "What if you or they hurt your backs or have a heart attack?"

When Nate and Addie adopted Hannah as an infant, they had never pursued finding any of her relatives. Addie had limited information from the adoption agency about Hannah's birth mother. She did not know if Hannah had ever wondered about it, but since Hannah had never asked, the subject remained unaddressed. Neither she nor Nate knew about a family member in

England who claimed Hannah was his sole beneficiary, whatever that meant. They didn't tell Hannah about their communication with Graham Pauly right away; at first they thought it was a bizarre scam, an elaborate prank. Naturally, as they later learned, Graham had initially contacted Hannah, as she was the client. Since then, Nate, Hannah, and Addie all felt excitement and trepidation about possibilities and potential pitfalls.

Upon returning home, Addie's childlike anticipation of discovery was palpable. She ran up the narrow, creaky stairs. When she reached the top step, it creaked, like it always did, reminding her that the house, although well-constructed and beautifully built, was quite old. It was a good thing they had kept the chest downstairs. Besides, it suited her personality. Addie loved old things, and the history and legends accompanying them. The chest was magnificent, and would have been perfect as a lovely coffee table, a conversation stopper.

Excitedly, Addie bounded into Nate's office and found him at his desk, his back turned to the door. She could see he was in the middle of stacking files and receipts. As a construction supervisor, Nate worked full-time restoring old estates on Long Island; one reason they were able to live in the Cold Spring Harbor house. Never would they have been able to afford a home so grand had it been in pristine condition.

"Nate," Addie said, "Have you looked at the chest?"

"Hi, honey. Yes, I have," Nate replied absentmindedly, bending over to search for something in a stack of files on his desk.

"Did you call Hannah and tell her it just arrived?"

"Not yet. Should we look through it first?"

"No, this is for her. I will call her and tell her it is here."

"All right."

"Aren't you excited?" Addie's intensity was comical. She chewed on her fingernails. "I mean, I still can *not* believe that Hannah is an heir to an estate."

"Addie, it could be a tiny estate," said Nate. "And it could be like this place was, in disrepair, when we purchased the property! Assuming that there is property in the estate…"

"True. The mystery is overwhelming, though." Addie added. She desperately wanted to go through the chest, but it belonged to Hannah, a gift from her benefactor.

Addie's childlike innocence and dependence endeared her to Nate. He enjoyed her unworldly nature and her capricious fascination with fashion and frills. Nate was a macho guy. He was not misogynistic but patriarchal, with a tendency to mansplain. But the paternalistic dynamic between him and Addie rarely caused any friction.

Addie looked at her husband, noting how very handsome he was. Over six feet tall, with a chiseled jawline, a trim, fit body, dark honey-brown eyes, and slightly graying deep brown hair, he looked regal even when wearing a hard hat, khakis, and a t-shirt on his construction jobs.

She picked up her phone and called Hannah.

"Hey, Mom, What's up?"

"It's here, Hannah."

"What?"

"The antique trunk from London."

"Mom, I'll come home for the weekend in a few weeks. I'm really busy until then."

"Hannah, prying it open will be quite a chore. Dad and I will start working on it and organizing its contents for you."

Hannah lost cell service and missed her mother's last comment.

Chapter 3: Letters

Hannah received a letter the day after the trunk arrived at her parents' home. She had never received a formal, elegant, yet oddly personal letter like this one. The envelope, addressed in looping cursive script, was written with a fountain pen, as if from another century. The embossed return address was from London, NW3, England.

When she opened the envelope, the paper smelled faintly of ink and tobacco. The penmanship was pristine, almost calligraphic. The letter was composed in the same elegant, fancy cursive script. Its message was brief, yet it changed something within her. She knew this was a watershed moment in her life.

The letter emitted a quiet gravity, as though it carried far more than words.

From: Mr. Zachary Levi

To: Miss Hannah Glass

Dear Miss Glass,

I hope this letter finds you in good health and a curious spirit. It is with warmth, and, I will admit, a touch of disbelief, that I write to you. Life has a strange sense of timing. Sometimes quiet. Sometimes symphonic. I am writing because we share a family connection that deserves a conversation. I realize this is unexpected and mysterious, but hopefully not concerning.

Please note that this is not an obligation, but rather an invitation. I offer it gently and without pressure. I am 94 years old, and time, while still generous, has grown more precious. If you are willing, I would be grateful to meet you.

Should you choose to visit me in London, my close friend and legal advisor, Graham Pauly, will help coordinate the details. He is clever, kind, and fiercely loyal. I suspect you will find him interesting and likable. So as to keep you in the loop, Graham can arrange a Zoom meeting for us to meet initially.

I wanted to let you know that we have shipped a chest containing facsimile ancestral diaries to your parents' home. They have been translated and transcribed from French, German, Polish, and Yiddish into English. The originals are being carefully digitized and archived by the National Library of Israel in Jerusalem. You will receive high-quality photocopies, fragile in their way but lovingly preserved.

Whatever you decide, I wish you clarity and peace in the journey ahead.

Warmly,
Zachary Levi

After reading the letter once, Hannah reread it. The loops of the handwriting were almost hypnotic. A family connection? Diaries transcribed and sent across continents? A stranger who claimed to share her bloodline? Hannah felt the thrill of mystery mingle with a pang of unease. The trunk and its contents had been intriguing enough on their own. Now, Zachary Levi added another layer to the enigma.

She laid the letter on the dining table, under the glow of the overhead light, and ran her fingers over the embossed return address. London, where Mr. Levi lived, claimed to hold answers. Why now? Why her? And why did his words feel like they carried decades of unsaid things?

Hannah gently folded the letter and placed it back into its envelope, her mind racing as she considered the implications. Her parents would want to read it, and would immediately start asking practical questions. But for Hannah, the questions were already much more personal. Could she face the truth if there was one? Could she enter a story whose opening act had been set long before her time?

The part of her that had always loved her parents' family stories felt a pull. Imperceptibly, her curiosity began to outweigh her hesitation.

She read the letter twice before responding, pleased to realize that she was unafraid. After much internal sparring, Hannah responded with her own letter.

From: Hannah Glass

To: Mr. Zachary Levi

Dear Mr. Levi,

Your letter arrived on an otherwise forgettable Tuesday, and I read it three times before I knew what I was feeling. I wasn't sure what to expect; certainly not a graceful, handwritten note from someone who says things like "curious spirit."

Yes. I would be honored to meet you. I have never received a gentle, elegant, precise letter like yours. It made me feel both known and completely unknown, which is a strange, yet not unwelcome sensation. I have often wondered about my ancestry, a mystery intriguing but impossible to solve, but I have never taken the time to explore it because my adoptive parents are incredible. I never want them to feel that they were lacking in any way.

Graham has already reached out. We have emailed, spoken, and met on Zoom. He seems genuinely kind. I will come soon. I have just started working on a fresh writing assignment, and I must do it justice before I disappear across the ocean.

Whatever this connection may be, I am open, eager, and honored to meet you and discover it.

I thank you sincerely for your invitation and this invaluable legacy gift. I wish you good health and look forward to meeting you soon.

Warmly,
Hannah Glass

After sending her reply, Hannah thought about Graham. Their first Zoom call two weeks earlier had taken longer than needed simply to make shipping arrangements. Their hour-long flirtation was fun and exhilarating, marked by an ease that lingered. She felt magnetically attracted to him.

He was ruggedly handsome, with a boyish cuteness. His voice was warm, and his smile broadened slowly, punctuated by a dimpled cheek that she found extremely sexy and irresistible.

Soon, their back-and-forth messages began. Two-hour Zoom meetings became a nighttime date-like regularity. Hannah started to reapply makeup at midnight in preparation.

"So, Hannah Glass. I assumed that was a pen name," he said flirtatiously.

Hannah said, "Nope. Real name, actual woman, major insomnia."

"That explains the 2 AM emails."

"What about your replies? Shouldn't you be getting ready for work at 8 AM in London?"

"Touché!" Her quick wit and sparkly giggle tickled Graham. *This woman has everything,* he thought to himself.

The next night, Graham sent her another video message. "How do you look like a French film star with only a ring light and an apartment plant?"

Hannah coyly replied that it was magic. "Also, Vaseline on the lens and years of unresolved trauma. And, of course, lipstick."

Graham guffawed with delight. "Irresistible combo."

"Confession," Hannah said, "I may have arranged the lighting like I was staging a boudoir scene or preparing a virtual date with a witty, handsome man. Your move, Pauly."

"How bold of you to assume I wasn't doing the same, with less success. Lighting is not kind to my thinning hair."

A few days later, Graham initiated their midnight Zoom call. "Can I say something possibly premature and uncool?" he began sheepishly.

"You can try," Hannah said.

"You are amazing. I am trying not to come on too strong, but I don't want to pretend that what's happening between us feels ordinary."

"It is not uncool, and this does not feel ordinary. Something between us feels extraordinary," she replied.

"I admit I am taken with you, Hannah. I am not looking for a fling. I am so done with casual encounters. You are on my mind all the time. I am falling in love with you. I cannot wait to meet you in person."

"That is wonderful news, and honestly, I can't believe I am saying this, but I feel it too. There is some serious chemistry between us." Hannah practically pinched herself with delight and thrill. She had to call Lucy immediately and tell her she was falling in love with a man in London.

Lucy, Hannah's best friend, was a character and hilarious. A banker on Wall Street, she was super bright and sassy, with a wonderful sense of humor, albeit with a sadness beneath it all.

"Hannah!" Lucy exclaimed, "How can you fall for a guy in another country who you haven't met? How do you know he does not have bad breath, smell, or wear sandals with socks?" They had a good laugh, and that was that.

Later that night, Hannah sat cross-legged in the bathtub, letting the steam rise around her. She did not write or think. Something strange and soft had settled in: hope.

Chapter 4: Between Us (*Entre Nous*)

Although the chest had arrived weeks earlier, Hannah's parents still had no idea what was inside, and neither did Hannah. She had not disclosed to them her correspondence with Zach Levi in London, nor mentioned the increasingly frequent phone and video exchanges with Graham. It was not that she intended to keep secrets; instead, it seemed only natural that she would be the first to explore the contents of a package sent to her on behalf of a man she had only just learned was a relative. This was, after all, Hannah's life unfolding.

Now the idea of the trunk made her nervous. It reminded her of her mixed feelings about wanting to learn about her history. She was afraid that the truth might be painful. On the one hand, she was curious; on the other, she was scared to learn why her natural mother gave her up for adoption. The trunk reminded her of the box of letters labeled "From Ella for Hannah" that Addie gave her when she turned 21. Years later, Hannah could not approach the box, still unopened, on the top closet shelf.

After its arrival, Addie treated the unexplored chest with reverence. For days, she hovered nearby, dusting it carefully, arranging fresh flowers near its base, and lighting a candle whose yuzu citrus scent lingered in the corners of the sunroom. She moved about as though preparing for a ritual, not one of religion or superstition, but something quieter and deeply personal. Her imagination had taken flight: she envisioned heirlooms wrapped in velvet, bejeweled tiaras hidden in secret compartments, or perhaps a rolled parchment sealed with wax, concealing a treasure map or a confession of love. *Pirate's booty,* she joked to herself, but she meant it more than she realized.

From the hallway, Nate observed her with quiet affection. He had always admired this part of her—the childlike hope, the capacity for wonder, the way she infused meaning into objects others would overlook. "Are you sure you don't want to peek inside before Hannah comes?" he asked gently.

Addie turned to him, her eyes bright. "No. It belongs to her. But I keep thinking, what if there is something remarkable inside? Something that changes everything."

Nate crouched beside the chest, inspecting its craftsmanship. As a skilled woodworker, he noted the dovetail joints, the hand-planed surfaces, and the finely etched bronze studs along the edges. The chest was no factory-made relic; a master craftsman had made it by hand, with care, and it had endured centuries. Judging by the decorative motifs and construction, he suspected it was French, mid-17th century. It had a quiet dignity, as though it carried its own memories.

Then Addie noticed something on the rusted lock. "Nate," she said, her voice unsteady. "Come here."

He joined her on the floor, where she pointed to a small inscription. "Look at this. It says, *Entre Nous.*" She traced the tiny engraving with her finger. "That is French. It means 'between us.'"

Nate raised an eyebrow. "Interesting. That confirms it originated in France and was once owned by someone French."

"It is the fourth time I have seen that phrase this week. Once on a postcard, once in that article about mother-daughter bonds I clipped for Hannah, and again on a tin of herbal tea I picked up at the co-op." She looked at him, her face suddenly serious. "Isn't that strange? It sounds silly, but I think it is a sign."

Nate did not laugh. He placed his hand on her back. "Maybe it means this chest is part of something meant for us or Hannah."

When Hannah arrived that Friday evening, Addie wasted no time. She practically pulled her daughter toward the sunroom. "You have to open it," she said, unable to catch her breath. "It's calling to us."

Hannah knelt beside the chest as Nate unlatched the brass hooks, which creaked with the sound of age. The scent of cedar and old fabric rose as the lid opened, revealing a haphazardly packed collection of items wrapped in linen and faded tissue. Nate stepped back and gestured. "It's all yours."

Addie circled the chest again.

"It's strange," she said, almost to herself. "This man you've never met, leaving you all this?"

"He hasn't left me anything yet," Hannah replied, trying to sound amused.

"Apparently, he does not have any family," said Addie.

"It is just you. Some people might wonder why he is including you now. They may think you are a gold digger or an opportunist. Just be aware of that." Nate said emphatically.

Hannah shrugged and rolled her eyes dismissively, but her stomach tightened. The exchange stayed with her, gnawing beneath the surface.

Addie could not help but resist, so she lowered her knees and reached inside the chest. She retrieved a small inkwell, a silver bell, a set of Meissen figurines, a handmade and intricate quilt, and, beneath it, an apron delicately embroidered with tulips and pansies, the edges worn soft with age.

Addie held the apron to her chest. "This looks so much like my great-grandmother's apron. She was 16 when she married. We have a photo somewhere—remember? With the embroidered roses and peonies?"

Nate shrugged. "I remember she lived to 97. Married in 1881, wasn't it?"

Addie nodded, her voice trembling. "She was a child, indeed."

Addie continued pulling out one thing after another, asking many questions about each item.

Hannah's patience was waning. "Mom, you are ransacking the contents! Take a chill pill and relax! These things are for me!"

Addie's mood shifted between Hannah's upset and Nate's relative disinterest. He didn't ask questions or marvel over the objects. Instead, his eyes drifted to the bottom of the chest, where a stack of neatly bundled folders, wrapped in archival paper and tied with string, lay in black velvet.

Hannah reached for one of the folders. "These are facsimiles," she said after a moment. "They are high-resolution scans. Somebody went through a lot of trouble to preserve the originals."

Addie blinked. "No heirlooms? No jewelry?"

Frustrated by her mother's materialistic focus, Hannah quipped sarcastically, "Nothing of value. Just history."

Hannah did not say what she was thinking. Her mother's obsession with signs and symbols, like the engraved phrase on the lock, made her feel disconnected. Addie always jumped to the most unscientific conclusions, as if the universe had time to whisper cryptic French messages into her daily errands. Hannah had spent years trying to rise above that kind of magical thinking she now eschewed. She felt guilty for being so snippy and haughty. But watching her mother now, wide-eyed and hopeful, she cringed at her mother's melodramatic antics. Hannah felt the old ache, a painful mix of embarrassment and protective love. She wished her mother were a woman who exuded depth and rigor, who grounded her and did not reach for cosmic meaning in a coincidence.

The weight of disappointment hung thickly in the air. Addie felt dejected and hurt by her daughter's critical commentary. She diverted her attention to the stuff in the trunk to console herself and soothe her wounds. As she rummaged through the chest, she wondered aloud: "Who had made the quilt? Who did the silver bell belong to? Who owned the Meissen figurines and the German beer steins?" She had allowed herself to believe in buried riches, in a fantasy that the past could hand her something glittering and real. Instead, they had been given stories; pages and ink.

Addie's voice dropped. "I suppose I was hoping for something more."

Hannah reached for one of the bound volumes embedded in the lining. It was fastened securely and it took effort to free it. At last, she lifted it and turned it over.

The cover read:

Countess Madeleine du Beaune
Journal 1643 Years After the Death and Resurrection of Our Lord

Hannah opened the voluminous journal. From a silent perusal of the first entries, she gleaned the voice of an articulate, sane woman in imminent danger. Madeleine's writing pulsed with intelligence, irony, and wisdom for a young woman of that era. She wrote of healing tinctures, moon cycles, and the science of plants; Madeleine was telling a story meant to correct and outlive accusations and condemnation.

Hannah felt captivated by the first passage: "If this diary survives me, know I am not a witch. I am a woman who loves and heals. I am a midwife who delivered babies into this world and held the hands of their mothers as they screamed. I am a steward of herbs and memory. They called me a sorceress because I knew the names of plants, read Latin, lived alone, and refused to marry again. I am a recusant being who belongs to the women. I still do."

Hannah made a mental note to research 17th-century witch hunts in France, an abjectly foreign subject that seemed highly disconnected from her own life. Yet the Countess also seemed a kindred spirit. She was feisty, outspoken, and stubborn. *There is something to chew on,* Hannah thought.

Nate tilted his head. "What's on the second?" Addie found it easily.

The Yellow Diary
1945
France

Addie's breath caught. A yellow Star of David, outlined in black, was stitched onto the cover. The word *Juif*—Jew embroidered above the star stood out in a harsh, Gothic font.

She gasped. Tears sprang to her eyes. "This must be from the war. It looks like it is the diary of a Holocaust survivor."

Nate nodded solemnly. "The Nazis reintroduced the Jewish Yellow Star badge in 1939. It was not new; Jews were mandated to wear identifying markers as early as the 13th century. But in 1941, with the invasion of the Soviet Union, it became systematic. Anyone who refused to wear it was punished or killed."

"The Nazis resurrected this practice as part of their persecutions during the Holocaust," Addie said.

Nate, a World War II buff, interrupted Addie. "Shortly after the Germans invaded Poland, the authorities enforced the mandatory wearing of the yellow Star of David badges. The Nazis applied this requirement to newly conquered lands. The German government's mandate of forcing Jews to wear the yellow star was but one of many propagandist and scapegoating tactics aimed at isolating and dehumanizing the Jews of Europe, directly marking them as being different, even subhuman. They also had different colored badges for homosexuals, for disabled people, and Roma. They branded people they considered inferior and worthy of extermination. All Auschwitz inmates were branded with numbered tattoos on the arm. They also gave the SS officers a tiny, hidden identifying tattoo; should their identity ever come into question, they would have proof of their loyalty to Hitler."

Addie ran her fingers over the embroidery.

"Yes," said Nate, "it allowed for the facilitation of their separation from society and subsequent ghettoization, which led to the deportation and murder of six million Jews."

"So much cruelty embedded in a symbol," Addie chimed.

Nate leaned in. "It is strange. Two diaries, from entirely different eras, stored together. If they made it here, maybe the writers were related."

Hannah said nothing. She had already begun reading, her attention rapt, and her face unreadable.

The chest had not delivered a string of pearls or a golden pendant, but it had given them something far more enduring: memory. It was not pirates' gold; it was a legacy.

And that was the end of it. The chest became a fixture, not just of the house but of the family's story. It held memories of ancestors, the weight of survival, and a reminder that what endures is not gold or gems but memory. Like all objects, the chest would one day rot, be sold, or be overlooked. But the stories might live on.

Nate stood, placing a hand on Addie's shoulder. "This is the treasure," he said. "The stories we tell and make our story work to our benefit. What survives is not what shines, but what is remembered."

Wasn't that the point of it all?

Chapter 5: Hannah's Diary

Hannah parked in her favorite Greenwich Village Café, La Lanterna, on McDougal Street. She opened her diary file and typed on her MacBook Air:

I am on my third espresso. It is raining outside, which feels right, in sync with my gloomy mood.

Who Am I? My name is Hannah Glass. Journalist. Traveler. Observer of people and the wreckage we carry.

I am 34. I am single. I have had my share of brief flings; some had beautiful moments, but all were meaningless. The kind of sex you barely remember and the men you try to forget. I have never been married. I do not have children. I have never fallen in love again. Not because I did not want to, but because I could not risk surviving another loss.

My parents wish I would settle down. They do not know I sometimes wake up, heart racing, not knowing why. That fear comes uninvited and stays too long. It always has. For years, I have wondered why I carry a vague sense of dread, a persistent free-floating anxiety that has outlasted lovers, therapists, and multiple brands of coffee and ice cream.

Addie, my adoptive mother and the only mother I know, used to say I was "born serious." She meant I looked worried, even as a baby. She once told me she constantly checked my bassinet because I never cried.

"Is that a trauma response? Not crying?" I asked Dr. Berman, my last therapist, and he said, "Maybe. Or you were observing the world. Some babies are quiet. Is it possible that your mother's anxiety is what brought her to check on you so frequently? That could have a direct effect on a baby!"

I have always been anxious. I was born predisposed to anxiety. I bite my nails and pick at my cuticles. My second-grade teacher called me a nervous Nelly and a Worrywart. Those epithets made me nervous because I did not know what they meant. My mother, Addie, calls anxiety "the family temperament." If that is the case, how does this work? Are my panic attacks a result of how I have been mothered? Is this how I have adapted to being adopted? Or is it biological? Genetic? The answer is both. It is not nature or nurture. They feed each other in a back-and-forth complicated loop.

As a journalist, I have written about science and psychiatry, grief and wonder, loneliness, and resilience. The stories have different names and settings but always circle back to the same truth: we need to love and serve something greater than ourselves. That is what makes us human. That is what keeps us alive, even when we feel shattered.

I believe 9/11 woke me up to the pain of the world. It was more than shock, it was something cellular, a recognition as if I had always known this terror, even before it happened. I could not name it, but it became part of my essence. Understandably, my anxiety got worse after 9/11.

I was a teen when the planes struck the Twin Towers. Several years later, David, my fiancé, was killed by a city bus. One moment, he was crossing the street; the next, he was gone. No warning. No goodbye. The scene, although unbidden, thrums in my brain at any time of day or night.

Is that why pedestrians walking on the street were screaming? A wild, untamed sorrow tried to consume my body. Fear. Fear was out there—and somewhere in here, within me. And everyone "out there" was reaching out with their minds, trying to connect to me.

Large and monstrous terror was hurling towards me in slow motion from somewhere. I was living a horrible dream, but what was it?

I wanted to escape.

"Someone, please call an ambulance!" The voice was muffled. "It hit him! It hit him!" another person yelled. "What?" I formed the words but was unsure if anyone could hear me.

I could not move.

If I shut my eyes and open them again, I might see a new reality.

The crowds were noisy. Full of chaos. And screams.

"Ma'am, were you with this person? Do you know who it is?" A woman grabbed my arm.

I could see nothing but blurs and shadows, and I was overcome with numbing fear.

The police shouted to get away from the accident. I heard an officer giving orders. Out of the corner of my eyes, I could see that they had set up flares along the scene's perimeter, instructing cars and taxis to turn back. The police closed the road.

The sun beamed softly and warmly on my body, but fear and disbelief struck me in the chest, where cravings and longings lay dormant, where ghosts lie dormant.

Earlier that morning, the May sky was full of promise, with a canopy of bright blue and the air cool and refreshing as the wind whipped through the Manhattan streets. I was hopeful about my present and future life with my love, David. We had officially announced our engagement, and my parents were planning a wedding in the summer at their home on Long Island. Those dreams were crushed in a second, snuffed.

Wearing a T-shirt and some leggings, I walked with David past the bodegas and jewelry shops with my feet in Nikes. We laughed and talked about our wedding plans and our future life. We had been in no hurry, which was unusual for anyone on the streets of New York. David and I even turned off our phones and put them in our pockets, both content to unplug for a few moments and soak in the golden rays. It had been raining, so when the sun peeked through the clouds, even for a moment, it was a call for a little celebration.

While walking with me across a crosswalk in downtown New York City, David was struck by a vehicle. Not by a bike, a motorcycle, a scooter, a car, an Uber, or one of the many taxis that zip through the streets. No. Not that. It seemed unthinkable—a bus. We neared a crosswalk, stepped to the curb, and looked both ways. I checked again and then again, and the Walk Sign blinked on.

We headed across the street. Happy. S-c-r-e-e-c-h! WHAT?

The sirens from an ambulance rang out from somewhere nearby, and a dog barked in the distance. I wanted to reach down, hold David, and pull him close.

Was he OK.? Where the hell did that bus come from? Then, a voice.

"Back off, everyone. Give us some space!" The medic's voice boomed in my ears. I had to face this reality when the paramedics pronounced him dead and laid a sheet over David's mangled body.

An extraordinarily terrible, tragic thing happened on an ordinary day. While crossing a street in downtown New York City, a bus struck David, killing him instantly. .

My world changed. My orbit changed. In one second, our dreams were smashed, left to gather dust and cobwebs in a grave, along with all the other souls of yesterday.

It has been a long recovery, but these events impacted me and how I approached the world. I was a fearful person before these events. My family and friends excused me from engaging with and relating to others for a long time. I hid behind my grief and kept it lingering as an excuse not to re-engage with my closest relationships.

Chapter 6: The Yellow Diary 1

"You need to have some time alone with these diaries," Addie said. "These are intimate things from your family's past; they are private and belong to you."

Hannah shook her head. "Mom, you, and Dad are my family; I do not consider this a secret. It is like I am looking at someone else's life. Not mine."

"We're all connected, honey," Addie said. "Your dad and I have some errands to do. We will be back soon."

They were downplaying this, but Hannah knew they were as shocked as she was about this delivery, and learning that she was the sole heir to someone's estate.

Hannah had not known what to expect when the trunk arrived, just that it had traveled far and carried weight beyond its size. The diary was inside, wrapped in parchment and tied with faded ribbon. A woman's handwriting, careful and slanted, filled its pages in two languages. The pages looked brittle, their edges browned with time, but Hannah held them like living skin. The copy was clean and modern, neatly translated, but beside each page was a facsimile of the original, the old German script in faded ink, the yellowed paper touched by the girl, Maria, who wrote them.

Hannah sat on the sofa in her parents' Long Island home, in front of the antique mahogany chest, and hugged her knees, the diary balanced on a pillow in her lap. Outside, spring rain tapped against the window. Inside, time folded.

Her shoulders hunched as she wept, the diary of an unknown ancestor trembling in her hands. She intuited something deep in her gut; Hannah did not know who Maria was. Not officially. Not biologically. But she felt it. Her chest tightened when she saw the way the girl formed her letters, how she crossed her t's like a musician pressing strings. There was artistry even in her pain.

Hannah sobbed, reading the *Yellow Diary* from Maria, who was somewhere in Germany. It was the first thing she opened after her parents unpacked the chest Zach Levi sent from London.

Yellow Diary Excerpts

(Translated from the original Yiddish and German manuscript, circa 1943)

April 3, 1943

I think we are somewhere outside Radom. I no longer ask questions about where we are. It is safer not to know.

I have not written in weeks or months. Time slips sideways here like a shadow, trying to remember in which direction light used to fall.

The cellar is narrow. We sleep in shifts. One lies down while the others sit. I have learned how to stop coughing with my mouth closed. I have learned how to forget what it feels like to be clean.

Today, I had a dream about my mother. She was wearing her embroidered apron with the tulips on the hem, standing in our kitchen with a bowl of peeled apples. I woke up with the smell of cinnamon and the taste of salt.

Salt from my tears. They came before I could stop them. I wiped them on the inside of my skirt and told myself it was only a dream, only an old dream.

What I want to say, what I must say—is this:

I have not died yet.

I am still here.

Someone must know that.

November 17, 1943

They came for the Groch family two nights ago. I heard the boots in the yard, the dogs, the woman's screaming. I did not look. I have learned that looking turns you into a witness. And witnesses are dangerous—they carry the dead inside them.

I am still at the farm. The woman here, Zoysia, lets me sleep in the barn loft. She says she once had a sister with "eyes like mine." I do not ask what happened to her sister.

I braid my hair tightly every morning to keep lice away. I wear my father's old coat. It smells of earth, tobacco, and something gone that was my father's smell.

Zoysia gave me a false name to memorize: Helena Kowalska.

It is a good name. Round vowels. Easy to say. I practice it in my sleep.

I write this by candlelight. The air in the barn is thick with hay and frost. I still have the small pencil I took from the schoolhouse the day it closed. Writing feels like breathing in a mirror—proof that I was once here.

August 9, 1944

I am in Germany now. Near a factory—I think. We have not been informed of the town's name. The guards speak quickly and only in shouts.

They packed me into a cattle car with dozens of other Jews. Two women died during the journey. One of them, I think, was only 16.

We are housed in a work barracks with stone slabs, shared blankets, and a tin bowl we use for washing and eating. The woman next to me hums at night. I do not know if she is praying or remembering a lullaby.

Every morning, we are marched across a dirt field to a large shed where we sort metal scraps. My fingers bleed from rust and wire. I have stopped feeling pain as usual—it now arrives as heat, cold, or the sudden absence of breath.

I have not said my real name in over a year. Last night, in the dark, I whispered it to myself. It felt like a betrayal, like calling out to someone who no longer exists.

March 4, 1945—Somewhere near Berlin

I am still alive. I do not know how. The Russian soldiers came again last night. I do not remember what happened, only that it ended with silence. And the way the rafters creaked afterward, like they, too, had survived something unspeakable. I lie still for hours. I do not cry. I will not give them that.

There was a woman in the village who tied herself to a tree. A Jewish woman like me, hidden for too long, starving for too long. They said she walked upright silently, wrapped in her mother's scarf. She did not leave a note. Only the image remains—her body swinging, almost still, like a warning or a prayer.

I keep seeing her not just in memory but in dreams. And sometimes, I wonder if it would be easier to join her. But then I remember the girl I once was—the girl who learned Chopin by ear, who danced barefoot in her father's orchard.

I am not ready to leave her behind.

Hannah stopped reading. She traced the word *orchard* with her fingertip. There was something unbearably delicate about how Maria moved between horror and memory, between terror and beauty. She turned the page.

March 12, 1945

The priest's wife gave me soup today. She knows I am not who I claim to be. I see it in her eyes. But she also knows what the soldiers do to girls. She said, "There is a reason you are still here. Do not forget that."

I no longer believe in reasons. Only choices. And the absence of them.

Hannah exhaled. Her fingers were trembling. She placed the diary beside her and curled up into a ball. *How do you read someone's suffering without absorbing it into your blood?*

She thought of the wailing baby in the house, a recurring dream. The cries behind plaster and brick, always muffled, never answered. She had dreamt it long before she touched the diary and heard Maria's name. And yet here it was—Maria's voice, buried and crying out.

She picked the diary up again and flipped to the pages marked in pencil by the archivist or a previous reader. One of them was titled "The Hanging Tree."

May 3, 1945

They call it liberation.

I call it something else. The after death.

The Russians arrived last week. We heard the shelling for days— deep rumbles like God grinding his teeth. When they came, they were drunk or broken, or both.

I began drawing faces on the wall to prove I still existed, had a name, and was once a girl who read novels, kissed in alleyways, and believed in living in Paris after the war.

They gave us bread, then took what they wanted.

I will not write the rest now.

What happened is still inside my body. Writing it would pin it to the page. That feels worse than silence.

I thought the worst was over. I thought surviving meant the end of fear. But it is not over. Not for girls like me. Not for women without men. Not for bodies already marked by too many hands.

I do not know what I believe anymore.

Only this: I am not what they did to me.

May 5, 1945

Once again I drew pictures on the wall. I want to see if I can feel, to know if I am alive and can think for myself. I want to believe in my life away from here.

May 10, 1945

A man came to the camp today. He was Jewish—he wore a pin on his lapel with a lion and a menorah. He spoke Yiddish, then German, and finally English. He asked if we needed anything. I did not talk. I could not. But I looked at him, and he saw me.

The man gave me clean socks, a tin of salve, and a bar of soap. He did not flinch when he saw my hands. He printed my name—Maria—as if it mattered. I may speak again tomorrow.

July 3, 1946

I think of my grandfather, Lev, who was beloved by many. He was a wonderful man, a humanitarian well-known throughout our village for his generous spirit and virtuous deeds. During the war, he single-handedly tried to save many families who were on the brink of being discovered and murdered by the German SS. Lev knew of an underground tunnel, and he orchestrated the arrival of dozens of people, 100 souls, shoved into the earth. The SS were above ground, looking for these people. They were out there with their dogs, sniffing and barking, screaming, letting the Jews know that they would be found and executed.

A young mother was unable to calm her wailing infant. Many people thought the same, but no one dared stifle the baby. Lev smothered the wailing baby to ensure the survival of dozens of other people. Hours later, the Nazis found them and executed all of them. I wonder if I will ever sleep without that cry in my ears. In my dreams, I still hear it. But I am determined that yesterday will not haunt me in America. Yesterday sleeps so that I can wake up.

Chapter 7: Yellow Diary 2

London, March 17, 1948

Today is the first time I am telling what they did to me a few years ago, towards the end of the war:

The Russians invaded Berlin just a few weeks ago, and chaos has reigned since. I made it through the entire war, hiding and running like a feral animal while my parents were murdered. I was about to die when liberation by the Americans was imminent.

A decent farmer let me hide under the cow's drinking trough in the barn, where they had dug a trench. Where were the farmer and his wife now? Did they kill them? The Russians ransacked the farmer's house, took his money, jewelry, and clothing, and set up an encampment within the home as if this were their new command center.

They did not know I spoke Polish and Russian, only that I was a German Fräulein.

Outside, the sunshine was comforting on my face. The hill country lay still in the early morning silence—a hollow quiet with only the rustle of wind amongst the apple trees and tall grasses. I imagined that the farmer and his wife had lived there before the war and spent many hours sitting on the front porch in the early morning or at dusk with coffee, tea, and biscuits. It was such a pleasant thought and alien to the moment. But I thank God for my vivid imagination; I would not have survived these years without it.

I was dirty, starved, and exhausted. I do not know how long I stayed in the ditch, silently screaming. My feet had cuts and blisters. I could feel my hair move from the lice that infested it. I was skeletal.

We walked to the farmhouse, a crumbling, rickety shambles with cobwebs in the rafters. I noticed a trapdoor on the floor. I imagined the farmer and his family often hid in the old building to escape the bombs. If they are not dead yet, they will be soon for hiding a Jewess.

Then one of the soldiers shouted in English, "Strip!" as he motioned for me to take off my clothes.

I stared at the men with a blank face, not showing emotion. It was with great determination that I would not give them the satisfaction of reacting.

Something was wrong with our world. I was not quite 15 years old. The world had gone wild.

"Strip!" the Russian soldier screamed. I pretended I did not understand what he was saying. I was so scared; my legs wobbled like a newborn calf, and my teeth chattered together.

I closed my eyes. The soldier ripped open my tattered dress, and it fell to the floor in a pile around my ankles.

I stood there, Skin and bones.

There were several of them—Russian soldiers. I do not remember how many. My mind has blurred the details, not out of mercy but from shock. They forced me down. Held me. Took turns. My body was no longer mine. Someone propped me up against the table and raped me from behind. They were laughing, passing around a cigarette. One of them looked barely older than a boy. One by one, they ravaged my body. They swore and screamed like banshees. I only remember feeling the searing pain of being ripped apart.

What they did lasted a long time, or maybe it felt that way. I floated above my own body, watching like a spirit. The only sound I remember is the squeaking of boots and someone muttering in a language I did not understand. It felt as though my back was breaking. They drank vodka, and they laughed.

An overwhelming terror overtook me. My memories are fragmented, unfocused, and beyond my ability to articulate.

"*Bitte*," I said in German. "Please. I am still a child." I was on the verge of giving up, and my consciousness began to fade. Degradation and dehumanization kill the soul.

I am shocked by the ways of sordid men, by the chaos, by the heinous cruelty that ordinary people engage in, and by what humans are capable of —the unthinkable and unnamable.

I do not know if it did happen that way. It is a blur, but that is what I imagine now when the sensations, anguish, and shock revisit me without warning, Horrific intrusions repeatedly. Again, and again, and again. Out of nowhere, these unwelcome scenes and sensations come to me as if they were happening then. I still smell the sour scent of vodka-tinged breath and sweat lingering from nowhere. The scent can be as strong as it was on that afternoon. The surge of nausea, palpitations, fear, and abject terror overwhelms me, and I tremble as if it is happening again. Consistently, I still check my nails for dirt, blood, and skin because my nails were ripped, broken, and bleeding from clawing at flesh and dirt to escape. I am afraid of everything, especially of men.

There is nothing noble in survival—only instinct.

I never told anyone about this. But the pain remained with me throughout my life.

The Hanging Tree

Hannah noticed that the pages were missing. Perhaps they never existed. Or Maria tore them out. But there is a faintly scribbled, barely legible note in the margin of the back cover:

They threw me in a ditch, leaving me there till the next day, when the men decided to hang me. They hanged me from a walnut tree. Someone cut me down. I never saw their face. I call them the angels.

That is how I survived. I write this now because I need someone to know. The details are not all that matters. It is also the silence afterward. The hunger is not only for food, but also for a good, kind word from someone, for some human connection: the shame and the terror. My body still flinches when a door slams, a train whistles, or a tap on the shoulder is perceived. The way I stopped singing with the sunrise.

To the girl who finds this, I hope your world is different. I hope you never feel the weight of your own body as something foreign. I hope your love is kind, gentle, and life-affirming.

Hannah read those lines twice, then a third time. She imagined the rope, the branch, the blur of sky, and the stranger's hands.

For the first time, she realized that Maria had not survived because the world was kind. She lived because only one person chose compassion and moral decency.

Hannah let the diary rest on her lap. Her palms were sweaty, her heart thumped, but her eyes stayed dry. It was too much to feel all at once. The words had entered her bloodstream.

Choking on her tears, Hannah calculated that it is only 9 PM in London. She logged on to WhatsApp to connect with Graham, who had quickly become a friend and confidant, and the man she was falling in love with.

Hannah began: "I just read something you should know about. Can I call you?"

"Of course," Graham replied, "I am home."

As soon as they connected face to face on Zoom, Hannah wept and told Graham, "I cannot wait to read more letters, more diary entries. I am spellbound by these letters. And I am heartbroken. And I don't even know the history of our connection."

He was alarmed to see her crying and asked her what had happened. She gathered herself and said she needed to know who Maria and Mr. Zach Levi were before going to England, because these diary entries unsettled her. "It's too much sadness and too much information to hold by myself," she said.

Graham tried comforting her. He told her that Zach had suggested disclosing to Hannah before her arrival that he was her grandfather, and that Maria was her maternal grandmother.

Hannah was stunned by the incredulity of not knowing her biological family. Her life seemed foreign to her, that her life narrative was ambushed, like a rug pulled from under her feet. She felt untethered, unmoored, and utterly bewildered, as if living in someone else's nightmare or dream. Graham listened, but all he seemed to be able to say was that he understood, and knew it was hard to grapple with earthquakes of this magnitude. That she could call him 24/7. That assurance made her feel better.

Learning that she had Jewish ancestry, that her grandparents were Holocaust survivors, also threw Hannah for a loop. The antisemitism craze in America and the rest of the world was not helping her absorb the news.

Graham reassured her. "Hannah, you'll be in London in just a few weeks. I want you to know you can lean on me, always."

"There's so much I didn't know," Hannah continued. "And now I am learning that my maternal grandparents are Jewish, which means I am not just emotionally and culturally Jewish, but biologically and genetically too.

Being Jewish feels like a big deal, and it matters to me more than I might have imagined."

Graham was quiet for a second. "That is big. But Hannah, you will adjust and grow from it all, and I will be at your side to help you."

This settled Hannah down at once, as it was the first bit of conversation with a future reference that left her feeling exhilarated. At the same time, she felt like Graham was already holding her close and protecting her, making it all better. She wished she could embrace him.

There was a pause, just long enough for the space between them to shift.

"I should probably say," Graham added flippantly, "I am not Jewish. I have no family history, no exposure beyond bagels and the occasional bar mitzvah at school. My parents were the 'High Church on Christmas Eve' type. They would have called this all exotic, I think. I'm not saying that exotic is anything bad," he said quickly, in an effort to gloss over the gaffe. "I'm trying to say that it's not something they knew about. Just that they inhabited a different world from yours. That's all."

Hannah's voice was quieter now. She was sensitive to the fact that Graham lost both parents to COVID-19 during the pandemic and did not want to start an argument. But the word "exotic" did not sit well with her; it seemed euphemistic for foreign and xenophobic. She felt numb.

"It is not just a world. It is who I am," she said softly.

"I know," he said. "And I want to understand. I do," Graham apologized.

She let that be the last word for now. But something in her stayed alert to the possibility that Graham was bigoted.

She also thought that someday, her children would know and connect to this history.

Chapter 8: Something in the Air

The café on Bleecker Street was half-empty, the way she liked it. Mornings were always best when the only noise came from clinking spoons and the hiss of the espresso machine, not from crowded tables or conversations loud enough to pierce her thoughts. Hannah took her usual corner seat, laptop open, not typing. Just watching the screen, cursor blinking, her mind somewhere else.

Hannah had a habit of working in cafés—not for the caffeine or the ambiance but for the illusion of structure and community. The people around her were typing, eating, sipping, and whispering, making her feel part of a species with routines. After four sips of her coffee, she was already deep into the world of Dr. Josephine Brightman, preparing for their first interview the following day.

The assignment had come quickly: write a long-form profile of Dr. Jo for *Currents,* exploring her work on trauma, legacy, and what she termed "emotional ancestry."

Hannah ordered Dr. Jo's book, *Yesterday Never Rests: How Integrating Past and Present Connections Improves Our Relationships and Our Lives,* the same night she got the pitch. It arrived the next morning in a yellow padded envelope, a paperback worn at the corners—someone else's used copy. She liked that it felt lived-in and authentic. She also invested in the Kindle version, in case she did not have the book handy and needed to reference it.

Her phone buzzed. It was a message from Lucy: "Did you see this? What the hell is going on at Columbia?" When Lucy left a message without cracking a joke, it was a serious matter.

Hannah clicked the attached link, and a video loaded showing students on the campus lawn chanting in unison, some holding signs that crossed the line from protest into something else. Something older. "Globalize the Intifada," one banner read. Another: "From the River to the Sea." The footage panned to a girl wearing a Palestinian keffiyeh, shouting that Jews were colonizers and murderers.

She had seen such things before, especially since the massacre in Israel on October 7, 2023. But it still shocked her how easily antisemitism had slipped back into the world, disguised now in the language of activism. She could almost hear her father's voice: "Hannah, it never really disappeared. It just waits for the right moment to come back in fashion."

Hannah and Graham had conversed briefly about antisemitism and Hannah being Jewish. Since the "exotic" comment, they tiptoed around the subject. Otherwise, they spoke about everything under the sun. They recently discussed Carl Jung's concept of the collective unconscious, which posits that memories are personal, cultural, collective, and encoded. That trauma does not vanish with time; it passes through families like a current, invisible but always humming under the skin, providing a constant foreboding experience.

Hannah closed the video. She felt exposed, even in this quiet café. Someone might see her and make assumptions, as if there was shame in being Jewish. Graham's comment about Jews being "exotic" was xenophobic. She was fretting and needed to calm down.

Hannah reminded herself that people do not only inherit unwanted emotional hand-me-downs. We gain their resilience, not just their fears. After all, the Jewish people have survived millennia of persecution. However, resilience and hyper-vigilance sometimes looked the same on the outside. And

Hannah hated how quickly she moved into defense mode now—how every protest, every meme, every offhand comment felt like a warning sign.

It was not rational. But it felt cellular and instinctive. Hannah's gut reactions to the news sometimes felt like déjà vu from a different era. That is how trauma works, she knew; it telescopes time. Hannah thought about that now. Time collapsing. The chants on college campuses felt like shadows of Kristallnacht. The Gaza war headlines read like repetitions of Warsaw. The caricatures in a new comedy show, "Nobody Wants This"—the "neurotic Jewish mom" trope, the cheap laughs at Jewish neuroses—did not feel harmless. They felt like warning flares. Time advances, but human nature is static.

Hannah glanced around. No one was looking at her, but she felt as if her self-consciousness was broadcast and widely visible. The first symptom alerting Hannah to an impending bout of anxiety was feeling her chest tighten and shortness of breath. She had read that the term for that familiar constriction in her chest is "dyspnea" or "air hunger," and can be a sign of hyperventilating, rapidly leading to lightheadedness. She was exhaling too much. A panic attack would ensue if she did not correct her breathing. She focused on moving the air slowly and more shallowly.

She stared at the cell phone screen. The latte before her went cold. Hannah successfully prevented a full-blown panic attack from declaring itself.

Having gathered her wits, preparing for the first interview with Dr. Brightman, Hannah flipped through her notes to review some key concepts:

Automatic Mental Construct—patterns of thought or behavior that once protected us now prevent us from seeing things. They are survival strategies that have become stuck in a loop.

Legacy Responsiveness—the way we respond to things, not because of what is happening now, but because of what happened to people before us. Trauma memory is not linear. It is sensory, buried, yet implicit. One can inherit someone else's silence.

Hannah found herself underlining sentences, not just because they were intelligent and informative, but because they struck a chord somewhere deep inside her. She wondered if Dr. Jo knew what kind of mirror she was handing readers.

She jotted down her thoughts:

What I am learning from all my research on the article I am working on is that our traumatic experiences live on in the body. Losing David was another rupture, another wound that never fully closed.

My adoptive parents raised me lovingly on Long Island. I grew up knowing nothing about my biological family—no names, no stories, just a silence that never stopped making noise in my body.

But recently, pieces started to fall into place. A connection to ancestors in 1600s France, Prague, and Poland. Traces connecting them in both World Wars. Whispers of women accused of witchcraft. Diaries written during times of terror and imprisonment. I began to understand that the panic and dread I carried might not have started with me.

Hannah was anxious and incapable of finding her footing after reading Maria's diary. However, she began to unearth a history that was not entirely hers yet embedded within her. She started to see how trauma does not disappear. It mutates. It hides in blood, brain, reflexes, and fear, passed down like a secret no one can reveal.

She opened some of her neuroscience notes, compiled from many articles, including some she had written for the "Mind Matters" column, and Dr. Brightman's book, *Yesterday Never Rests*.

Trauma's legacy can reshape the way brain regions communicate with each other.

The Inherited Imprint of Stress Hormones.

She thought again about something she had read in Dr. Brightman's book—how trauma can leave a biological residue, like soot on the DNA. Trauma does not just scar memory. It rewires the brain. Chronic stress and unresolved fear create neurochemical loops. Over time, the body adapts, but not as we had hoped.

Cortisol dysregulation, immune exhaustion, and insomnia—these were not just symptoms. They were echoes. Derivatives. Recapitulations. Evidence of something carried, inherited. Scientists now believe that trauma can leave its mark on DNA, not by changing the DNA sequence itself, but by modifying the surface of the chain known as the epigenome, tagging the surface through methylation, thereby turning stress into chemical memories. These tags could be passed to children and even grandchildren.

Hannah had underlined that part. She remembered thinking: *That is why the dread did not always feel like it belonged to me.* Living in the shadow of trauma meant recognizing the difference between fear that was earned and fear that was handed down. And seeing how those shadows shape our reactions. Even if you do not remember what happened to your grandmother, your *cells might.* Your breath. Your startle reflex. Your dreams. Hannah had wondered how she could be in a great mood and feeling well when, out of nowhere, panicky feelings erupted. Sensing impending doom, the need to escape wherever she was at that moment, her gut twisted into knots, and she felt lightheaded, faint, and experienced palpitations. What precipitated this cascade?

Then Hannah closed the laptop. And she just sat there, watching the steam from someone else's coffee, lost in reverie.

Looking out of the window, she noticed an elderly couple sauntering down the rain-dampened sidewalk. The man had a thick head of white hair and a proud handlebar mustache. The woman's curls framed her face, and she pushed her glasses up the bridge of her nose as the couple shuffled through autumn leaves, arm-in-arm. Occasionally, they paused to smile at a squirrel or a sparrow feeding near the curb. They did not seem to mind the wind or the gray skies. They were absorbed in conversation—and in each other.

Hannah nicknamed them Sally and Bob. She did not know why, but naming strangers brought her comfort. Watching them stirred deep within her a wistful and hopeful ache.

Would they tell her that love is less about finding perfection and more about building trust over time? Is intimacy found in the slow accumulation of shared mornings and hard conversations? She imagined them having survived wars, maybe even childhood heartbreaks, and still walking through life together, laughing, loving, and protecting each other from the cold.

What Hannah saw between them was not just affection. It was a lifetime of becoming. They had created a whole private world of alchemy with trust and rhythm.

Hannah longed to build something like that with someone, to find a life partner who would meet her in silence and speech, joy, and grief. She imagined Graham beside her—not just now, in the early heat of their infatuation, but years from now. Grown old together. Laughing together and still reaching for each other's touch without thinking. *Someday,* she thought, *let it be us.*

The rain had stopped. She dropped some cash on the table, grabbed her umbrella and bag, and stepped out into the city, still soaked with memory.

Chapter 9: The Interview

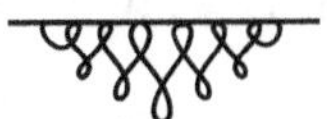

Hannah hesitated at the heavy wooden door on East 78th Street, smoothing her clammy palms against her jeans. Her stomach was in knots, too, more than it should be for an interview. A small brass plaque beside the door read Josephine Brightman, MD. *So, this is Dr. Jo's lair*, she thought, half expecting something intimidating. Instead, when she pressed the buzzer, a warm voice invited her in, and a lock clicked open.

Hannah entered a cozy waiting area with abstract paintings in calming blues and greens adorning the walls. She wondered how many people had passed through the waiting room, carrying invisible burdens. A woman immediately appeared from an inner office with a gentle smile.

"You must be Hannah. Come on in," said Dr. Josephine Brightman, extending a hand. She was in her mid-60s, a petite figure with silver hair swept into a loose bun. Inquisitive eyes sparkled behind trendy tortoiseshell glasses, and shallow crow's feet etched the corners. Hannah shook her hand, finding Dr. Jo's grip warm and steady. The older woman's presence was easy, professional yet surprisingly inviting. Tense with anticipation, Hannah realized she had been breathing shallowly. She sucked in a deep breath and exhaled.

"Thank you for making time for me, Dr. Brightman," Hannah said as she followed her into the office.

"Please, call me Dr. Jo," the doctor replied. "Everyone does."

The office did not look like the analyst's den Hannah had pictured—no clinical couch or ticking clock. Instead, it was a book-lined study with tall windows overlooking a pocket-sized garden courtyard. Sunlight filtered through the paned glass, creating a pattern of rectangles on a Turkish rug. Two plush armchairs faced each other across a low coffee table. Hannah noticed an old ceramic mug on the table, a wisp of tea steam curling from it. An abstract sculpture of a mother-child pair intertwined, tucked into one of the bookshelves. The space radiated comfort as if meant for intimate confessions or storytelling over tea.

She took a seat in the armchair, as Dr. Jo indicated. The cushions were soft and enveloping; she clutched a throw pillow to her midriff like a protective buoy. Hannah felt her heart thumping harder than it should for a professional interview. *Get a grip*, she told herself. She was here to do a job: a profile on this renowned psychoanalyst for *Currents* magazine. Still, a part of her wondered: *How will I distill all of this—the ambiance, this woman, and this weighty topic—into an article?* She silently repeated to herself to focus and stay on task. Yet "Telescoping Time"—the working title in her head for this piece—felt more personal by the minute.

Dr. Jo sat across her, smoothing her long skirt and crossing her ankles. "How shall we begin, Hannah?" she asked gently. "First meetings can be a little nerve-wracking, I know."

Hannah managed a self-conscious laugh. "Caught me. I am a bit nervous," she admitted. "I interview people all the time, but I don't usually do it in…well, in such a personal setting." She glanced around the cozy room. "This is much nicer than a sterile conference room."

"I'm glad you find it comfortable," Dr. Jo said. Her voice was low and soothing, with a trace of an accent Hannah could not place. "I promise I don't bite. And this doesn't have to feel like an interrogation. Think of it as a conversation. We are both just people, curious about people in our world, wanting to help or contribute somehow."

Hannah nodded and exhaled. The pillow in her arms began to feel less like armor and more like an old friend, or a lover.

"Thank you. I like that, a conversation," Hannah said while fishing for the digital recorder from her tote and setting it on the coffee table. "Is it OK if I record? So that I don't miss anything?"

"Of course," Dr. Jo replied. Then, with a light laugh, she added, "Just don't let the technology get in the way of us talking. If you want to go off record at any point, say so."

Hannah was surprised. Most interviewees insisted on recording essential points, but few offered to go off the record.

"Sure," she said softly.

She pressed the record button, saw the light glow, and then mostly forgot about it as she met Dr. Jo's attentive, searching gaze.

"I would like to tell you about me in two sentences," Hannah stated matter-of-factly. She did not want Dr. Jo to think she was an obnoxious braggart; she just wanted the doctor to know she was smart. Hannah mentioned graduating magna cum laude from Barnard with degrees in Creative Writing and Broadcast and Print Journalism, and that she had freelanced for ten years.

After a silent moment, she added, "Well, you know I'm here to discuss your background growing up with Holocaust survivor parents, inherited trauma, and all you've discovered in your practice. Let's start with an overview and your description of Psychological Intelligence.

"All right." Dr. Jo reached over to a side table, picked up her cup of tea, and took a sip. "I grew up with Holocaust survivor parents, so life was filled with echoes of trauma during my childhood," she said. "Throughout my years as a psychiatrist in practice, I observed how emotional trauma affected me, my patients, my children, and other loved ones. When a person endures a life-threatening trauma, the ghosts, hardships, and fears of their past increase present fears, causing more anxiety, depression, and moodiness. Children can perceive when a parent's behavior, language, demeanor, and general coping methods have been drastically altered. The effects could manifest as ongoing stress in their children and future generations."

"Your book, *Yesterday Never Rests*, moved me," Hannah replied. "How you describe trauma is surprisingly poetic for a psychology book."

Dr. Jo's lips curved in a modest smile. "Thank you. I wanted it to speak to specialists and ordinary people alike. Trauma isn't just a clinical thing; it's a human story."

Hannah relaxed another notch. Trauma was a topic she could engage with.

"One idea that struck me was your assertion that trauma never truly disappears," she said, glancing briefly at her notebook for the line she'd copied. "You wrote: 'Trauma is a ghost that doesn't fade away; it mutates and embeds itself, shaping how we love, how we fear, how we live.' Could you explain what you mean by that? For our readers, I mean."

Dr. Jo tilted her head thoughtfully. "I mean that harrowing experiences leave a kind of imprint," she replied. "Even when we think we've buried the past, it finds ways to resurface—sometimes in disguise." She leaned forward slightly, hands loosely clasped in her lap. "Picture a tree that's been through a harsh winter. It grows new leaves in spring, but its rings carry the memory of that frost. Similarly, a person may go on with life after trauma and appear to be fine, but that trauma has left marks in their psyche, even in their body. It might show up subtly, flinching at a loud noise years after a battlefield, or struggling to trust a loving partner because someone long ago betrayed you."

"I will tell you a story about myself." Hannah leaned in, listening closely. As Dr. Jo spoke, her voice soft but sure, Hannah's journalistic detachment gave way to personal understanding. She thought of her rings of the tree, the silent spaces in her childhood where her birth mother's absence lived, the raw wound left after her fiancé David's death years ago. She still sometimes reached for him in the dark, half-awake, before remembering he was gone. *Was that a ghost of trauma? A pattern shaped by pain?*

Dr. Jo continued, "In medical school, I knew I could never be a surgeon. I hated cutting flesh and doing invasive procedures. Years later, I realized that cutting didn't faze me, but cauterizing and the resultant smoke and smell of burnt flesh sickened me. I had an epiphany when my husband and I visited India."

"The embankment along the Ganges River in Varanasi, India, is the holiest burial place for Hindus," Dr. Jo explained. "The city skyline is dense with the smoke of cremated bodies. I was reminded of my late parents' description of pogroms, including the smoke from burning synagogues, books, and murdered corpses. *Holocaust survivors shouldn't be here,* I thought."

"We had carefully prepared ourselves with N95 face masks, hats, and goggles. Nevertheless, my senses were overloaded. My eyes stung, and my throat was raw. My pulse quickened as the sweet, putrid smell of burning flesh alarmed me, setting off traumatic iterations of millions murdered and burned in ovens." Hannah nodded.

"More than that, when I was two years old, in an infirmary to address an infected bite at a vacation resort, a sadistic nurse with a steaming metal iron seared my bottom. Held down and immobilized, I howled and screamed into a deafening silence as the tip of the scorching iron landed on my tender baby flesh. Into my young adulthood, I struggled with the sickly-sweet odor, visuals, and pain of burnt flesh, ashes, and anything barbecued." Hannah gasped in horror; at the same time, she was touched, and appreciated Dr. Jo's candor. She could understand the doctor's associating smoke and burning flesh in Varanasi to the smell of charred meat, and why it would be triggering.

"Before I made these connections, I experienced free-floating anxiety but didn't understand the links to my history, which puts the present day in perspective. In Varanasi, I categorized these associations and memories without angst or the physical stress response of my sympathetic nervous system, outpouring cortisol and adrenaline. I could experience it contextually as spiritual and sacred."

"It makes sense," Hannah murmured. "Painful experiences do not just vanish. They linger in our reflexes, even in our choices." She realized her guard was lowering faster than expected. Clearing her throat, she added, "But some people would say, 'Time heals all wounds.' Do you agree?"

Dr. Jo laughed gently. "I think time distances wounds, but healing is something else. Time alone can just as easily let wounds fester if we never address them. It is what we do at that time that matters." She paused, studying Hannah with a curious, kind gaze. "Sometimes wounds aren't even from our own lives. They can be handed down, like an heirloom."

This was edging toward the very heart of Dr. Jo's work. Hannah felt a familiar skepticism tug at her, a reflexive need to question bold claims. "You mean inherited trauma, right? Like something passed from parents to children."

"The term 'inherited trauma' is a mistake, or a misnomer. We inherit the effects of trauma, not the trauma itself," Dr. Jo said. "I call it emotional ancestry. We inherit more than skin color from our genes. We inherit the residue of our ancestors' experiences. One traumatologist calls it 'Embodied History.' Some historians refer to the way descendants feel as if they experienced the trauma directly as 'Post Memory.'"

Hannah tapped her pen against her notebook. "I must admit, I found that fascinating, but also hard to wrap my head around. How can someone inherit trauma if they never actually lived through it? Is it metaphorical, or literal?"

Dr. Jo seemed pleased by the question. "It's a bit of both. We don't inherit the memory of the trauma—at least not consciously—but we can inherit the fallout of it in our bodies and behaviors. She uncrossed her legs and sat forward as if eager to explain. "Research shows that severe stress can leave biochemical marks on DNA. It's called epigenetic change. In plain language, imagine stress leaving little Post-It notes on your genes, telling your body to be extra alert or anxious. Those 'notes' can sometimes be passed to children."

Hannah raised her eyebrows. The explanation was consistent with the scientific backing she'd read about but still found astonishing. "So, if a parent survived something horrible—war, famine, a horrific loss…."

"Their children might be born with a body primed to handle a world full of danger," Dr. Jo finished. "Even if the children grow up in peace and plenty."

An old memory of Hannah's father—her adoptive father, she reminded herself—fluttered up in her mind: he had been watching the news of yet another civil conflict. "It never really goes away, Hannah," he'd said, sighing about the hatreds of the world. "Trauma has a long shadow." At the time, she'd thought he meant historically. She now wondered if he had also meant something more personal, passed down in their family line.

"That sounds almost mystical, like ghosts in the blood," Hannah said slowly. "But I know you're talking about real biology. I came across a study you mentioned—about mice conditioned to fear a certain smell, and their pups who were afraid of that smell, even though they'd never encountered it with their senses."

Dr. Jo nodded, her eyes lighting up. "Yes! Exactly. Researchers introduced the scent of cherry blossoms to a group of mice and paired it with a mild shock. Eventually, the mice would get anxious just by smelling cherry blossoms. The incredible part? Their offspring, who were never shocked or trained, also showed anxiety when they smelled cherry blossoms. Somehow, the parent passed down a message: 'This smell is dangerous.'"

"Let's set genetics aside and focus on the direct impact a parent can have on their child," the doctor continued. "Let me highlight that young children can absorb a parent's intense emotionality by osmosis. Here is a personal, yet benign, case of a direct effect of parenting. My mother couldn't stand the scent of lamb meat. Any association with it made her nauseated. For some reason, until recently, I was convinced I hated lamb and wouldn't go near a lamb chop for decades. When I finally tasted the meat, I thought it was delicious! However, I still avoid the food, and my children rarely eat lamb."

Dr. Jo looked at her wristwatch. "Wow, these 90 minutes flew by. Let us continue with the epigenetics of inheritance the next time we meet. I look forward to seeing you in two weeks, Hannah. We will resume our discussion."

Chapter 10: Dreams and Genes

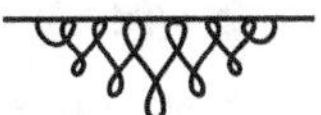

Hannah returned to Dr. Jo's office two weeks later with a different tension behind her eyes. She was carrying something—not physically, but emotionally. Dr. Jo sensed it as soon as Hannah walked in.

"You look a bit burdened today," Dr. Jo said, gesturing toward the armchair.

"Yes," Hannah replied, sitting down. "I've been reading *Yesterday Never Rests,* which I've got a copy of on my nightstand. It is dog-eared and highlighted to high heaven. The way you describe intergenerational trauma—it's like you put words to things I have felt but never articulated—especially the idea of being a proxy witness to our parents' and grandparents' stories.'"

"That means a lot to hear," Dr. Jo said. "When I wrote about being a witness by proxy—how children of trauma survivors carry stories in our bones—I hoped it would resonate for people exactly in your shoes. How would you describe what it meant to you?"

Hannah took a thoughtful moment. "I have inherited this bundle of feelings and half-told tales. My mom told me some stories, but so many things were unsaid. It always felt like an entire world behind her eyes that I could not see, but I thought it was there. Is that what you mean— being a proxy witness to their suffering?"

"Precisely. You're describing it well," Dr. Jo says with gentle enthusiasm. "It's like you have an emotional heirloom. Your family experiences were so powerful that even if your mother never fully shared them, they have been handed down in some form—not the memories themselves, but a reverberation, a resonance in you."

"Yes"! Hannah replied, "And sometimes I wonder, is it hers, or is it me making it up? Like a second-hand phantom of her trauma?"

Dr. Jo furrowed her brow, steeped in deep thought. "That is an insightful question. A lot of second-generation survivors—2Gs—whether of the Holocaust or other atrocities, feel that way. A mix of 'What do I truly feel?' and 'What have I inherited?' Often, present feelings are entwined with history; they are genuine in you, even if the origin of those feelings predates you. This gray zone of managing and distinguishing feelings of your own from those you've inherited is one area where narrative therapy can be beneficial. When we start telling the story of those feelings, we understand them better and sometimes change our relationship."

"Narrative therapy, as in shaping personal stories to heal?" Hannah asked, smiling.

Dr. Jo affirmed, "Yes. It is about authoring your story about your life, struggles, and family legacy. Creating our story and telling and retelling it in a safe space can be profoundly healing. The concept is consistent with Attachment Theory. People with good self-reflective ability who can create a wholesome narrative that is layered, nuanced, and constantly updated develop more secure attachments and have more social success across the lifespan."

"That reminds me of what you wrote in *Yesterday Never Rests*," Hannah responded. "About how you had to update your parents' narratives within your own life. To not betray their story but still live and tell your own."

Dr. Jo leaned forward. "You read my book closely. I had a hunch you might. And if you carry intergenerational trauma, there's a layer of protectiveness, too, isn't there? Your story might betray your family's privacy or break some unspoken code. Keep in mind that there's no right or wrong. Every generation wants their children to tell their family story just as they've told it themselves, but it's always modified because you're living a different life than your parents. Their environment, culture, and society were different."

She paused, studying Hannah. "My mother, for instance, was terrified of dogs because she was bitten by one, while you might be grateful to be around a dog because you may have had fun with them, or felt loved and protected. My mother would nearly faint when she saw police officers or uniformed officials, automatically assuming they were coming after her. In contrast, you might see men in uniform and feel grateful that they're managing difficult or dangerous situations. I grew up fearful of dogs and men in uniform as well. But I learned to manage my emotions."

"Yes. Like, I owe them silence as solace for suffering. Or I'll get it wrong, somehow." Hannah said.

Dr. Jo spoke softly, "That is a powerful statement, Hannah. Owe them silence for their suffering. Who comes to mind when you say that?"

Hannah reminded herself this was an interview, not therapy, and felt slightly uncomfortable. Still, she responded. "My Grandmother, mostly. And sometimes my mom. But my mom's different—she's more open, while Gran had so much, she kept it inside. I don't know. Now, I've just discovered from these letters and diaries that were mysteriously sent to me by a long-lost relative that I seem to have in London, that my natural grandmother was a tortured Holocaust survivor. It seems like both of my grandmothers had been to hell and back."

Hannah worried that delving into the whole story would derail her from the article she was trying to write.

"They both survived something harrowing, from what I gather." Dr. Jo replied.

Hannah spoke tentatively, choosing her words carefully. "Yes, Gran, um, she grew up during the rise of the Nazi Third Reich, such a dehumanizing regime. But she was my adoptive grandmother. Although she made it to

London on the *Kindertransport,* the early years of her life were scary, and she was still in an orphanage. That has something to do with my nightmares. Gran and I have both lived in orphanages; we share that, but at dissimilar stages and life circumstances. Also makes me wonder: can the emotional effects of trauma be inherited if someone's adopted? Can it be a relational event and not biological? I never thought of that until now!"

Hannah surprised herself by revealing this so soon. Dr. Jo, noticing the sudden vulnerability, kept a gentle calm. She nodded, "Would you like to tell me about it?"

Hannah seemed pensive for a moment. "There is one recurrent dream I have that makes me wonder; I'm in an old house that feels familiar, like my childhood home, except it's empty. And I hear a baby crying through the walls, whether in the basement or underground, I can't discern. Gut-wrenching. I can't get to it. And I always wake up in a panic, my heart racing. I endeavor to rescue the infant but can't find the right location. The panic I always feel in the dream is the same as what I felt reading the diary."

Jo listened without interruption. Hannah went on. "In Maria's diary—that's the natural grandmother, whose diary my relative sent me—there's this passage where she hears something—a muffled baby, imagined, maybe real. She was underground, and she talked about the need to keep silent, about what happens if someone makes noise. Here, I have it."

From her messenger bag, Hannah took out her copy of the diary, opened to a marked page. The Xeroxed copies of the original document lay to the left of the book's spine, whereas the right-sided pages were translated and transcribed. The paper was good stock printer paper. Hannah read a passage aloud softly. Then she decided to paraphrase it, because it was too long.

"Here is the passage: July 3, 1946. 'I think of my grandfather, who was underground with dozens of other Jews and had to finally smother a wailing baby to ensure the survival of the dozens of other people. The Nazis found them and executed all of them. I wonder if I will ever sleep without that cry in my ears. In my dreams, I still hear it. But I am determined that yesterday will not haunt me in America. Yesterday sleeps so that I may wake up tomorrow.'"

Hannah stopped, her voice catching slightly. Dr. Jo's gestures reflected empathy and interest. As the words settled in the room, Hannah hesitated. How could she write about something this important and this serious without reducing it? Was she exploiting ancestral pain and suffering for a story, or was she bearing witness? She thought, *Be sure to make this article about Dr. Jo and not about me.*

Dr. Jo reached for her teacup, then paused, glancing at Hannah with concern. "You know, I'm reminded of a patient I worked with, I am trying to remember, it's right on the tip of my tongue," she digressed, then, smiled sheepishly. "It's funny how the brain works; sometimes the most relevant point decides to hide. I can't remember what I was thinking," Dr. Jo said, her face flushed from embarrassment. "'Yesterday, I slept so that I may wake tomorrow.' Wow. And the crying baby. Understandably, Maria would want to heal from trauma. We can't blame her for that wish; however, the unconscious mind is timeless."

Hannah was momentarily distracted by Dr. Jo's memory lapse. *Naturally, she is not perfect,* Hannah thought. *She's human and fallible.* Her mind wandered to Addie. At that moment, she felt a tender longing for her mother when feelings of love, guilt, and remorse arose intermingled. She was aware of a lump in her throat and a queasiness. *I am annoyed, snippy, and mean to her when she gives me unconditional love and acceptance.*

Hannah's mental chatter continued with the realization that she unconsciously blamed Addie for her feelings of rejection and abandonment because Ella decided to give her up for adoption. It was the first time Hannah consciously considered this possibility to explain her behavior.

Hannah snapped back to the present: "I know. When I read that, my heart just skipped. I had no foreknowledge that she wrote that. But I do remember being freaked out when I saw the movie called 'Sarah's Key,' a story, based on the novel by Tatiana de Rosnay. It is in part about Sarah's attempt to save her brother, who died in the closet where she hid him, and she could not get back to save him because she was incarcerated. His skeleton was found in the wall decades later. These kinds of stories of trading lives for one another are quite common among Holocaust survivors, so I knew these tragic events were ripe ingredients for the dream. I have read a lot about passing judgment on people who had to do terrible things during unfathomable circumstances, and that we can't apply standard moral codes to people in 'Sophie's Choice' situations—those no-win predicaments, as in William Styron's novel."

"It's remarkable," Dr. Jo exclaims. "Your nightmare about the crying baby is written in your grandmother's diary. It may be a combination of 'Sarah's Key,' where the brother in the wall is involved, and your grandfather's underground rescue in a tunnel, when he smothered the inconsolable, wailing baby. These events seem powerfully linked to ancestral memories that have found a way into your subconscious. How do you feel when you read it? What do you think about when you read it now?"

Hannah exhaled slowly. "It feels validating, strangely. Like I'm not crazy. I have another thought, but I've never thought about this before. When I was very young, before we moved to the new house, I heard crying kittens outside my window at night, and I thought they were abandoned human babies. Maybe that also figures into it in some weird way, as the mélange of these different events converge. It feels like there is some fundamental connection in my stories. For example, I saw film footage of mass graves and heard stories of Jews trapped in buildings that burned, entrapped in the crematoria and the gas chambers, and cattle cars where they suffocated. And screams abounded. I probably heard a similar story about babies being smothered because it was not an uncommon occurrence, from what I understand. There were many 'choiceless choices' that no one should ever have to consider. I always wondered where my brain concocted that image. Now I know Gran's story and the Holocaust stories from my childhood. I thought of those cats as abandoned babies because that's what I heard around the house; after all, I was adopted and abandoned by my mother."

"You know," she mused aloud, "I never thought of this, but I was adopted at two months old. I was kept in an orphanage until then. Who knows how I was treated? Perhaps I was left to cry all day. My screams weren't heard! This may sound far-fetched, but maybe I was left in a crib all day and no one attended to me regularly or well enough."

"Wow, Hannah, those are important connections you are making," Dr. Jo replied. "You are right to consider that pre-verbal terror, or fear, or not being well taken care of, is encoded in the body. It's tough to speak before you can apply language to what you're experiencing. You are beginning to understand your nightmares and your anxiety."

"That brings me to some critical points about the unconscious mind relevant to this discussion," Dr. Jo continued. "Our unconscious steers us. The way we think is out of our control. The unconscious content gets connected to repetitive patterns of behavior, and we make the same mistakes repeatedly, unable to correct our thinking and behave differently. These become organizing principles that drive our behavior. You know, I called those Automatic Mental Constructs; AMCs. The unconscious does not have a physical location in the brain, but it shapes everything else, just as the sky covers everything without touching anything. The unconscious is timeless. It connects the past, present, and sometimes future. It contains the hidden memories, intense emotions we do not recognize, unexamined beliefs, unacknowledged desires, and longings rooted in our own experiences or those passed down to us by osmosis through the generations."

Hannah listened attentively and checked the recorder to ensure it was still on. Dr. Jo continued with her spiel, a brief monologue summarizing her stance.

"The more we understand ourselves and our inner thoughts, the better we can predict our future and manage our behavior. We will be less influenced by emotion and more able to use our sense of reason and rationality to control our words and actions; more able to be the person we want to be, empathetic and kinder. The more we know our unconscious mind, the more detailed and complete our life narrative becomes. We fill in the blanks and connect the dots. The puzzles are solved."

"Freud was right on target in *The Interpretation of Dreams*. He wrote that dreams are the 'royal road to the unconscious mind.' Freud proposed that dreams disguise our deepest desires, particularly those we cannot face in waking life. Dreams, he argued, draw on day residue—recent experiences or thoughts—and translate them into symbolic narratives. Decoding these elements, we access repressed emotions and conflicts that shape our waking behaviors. If we know ourselves, we can choose a better path. Since dreams tap into our deepest fears, longings, and wishes, they can help us shape our future direction."

"You received the story even if you don't remember hearing it. The brain, especially the emotional brain, holds so much that it isn't explicit memory. It's possible that you listened to it as a child, overheard a conversation, or someone mentioned it, and you were too young to grasp it fully at the time, so the memory was stored away until triggered by the right moment. Or, more mysteriously, it traveled through the family narrative in unspoken ways. Either way, it's part of what we meant by emotional ancestry. These things often come up in the context of something current that triggers memories and dreams."

Hannah, nodded in agreement. "Right. It makes me think of something you wrote about in *Yesterday Never Rests*: how trauma has a way of echoing, sometimes in whispers, across generations. Like a muted repetition that the next generation hears in fragments."

"We inherit not the horror but the reverberation of the intense anguish of the emotion," Dr. Jo stated emphatically. "The nightmare is like a repeat of your grandmother's lived terror. It can also have to do with your own life, as you said, like being in an orphanage for a few months when you were just born. Hearing abandoned cats outside your window as a small child could be scary, too. These experiences build on each other, creating anxiety. We don't necessarily have to invoke your ancestors. We have our issues and traumas in this life."

Dr. Jo continued, "Now, in narrative therapy terms, this could be an opportunity for re-authoring. You and I, in conversation, can help Hannah, the character, meet Gran and Maria, the characters, and rescue that crying baby—symbolically, I mean—so that your story, Hannah's story, can move from terror to empowerment. Does that make sense?"

Hannah took this in, nodding slowly: "It does. Is it like finishing the story differently?"

"Yes, finding a way to give it a new ending or meaning." Dr. Jo replied. Not changing the unchangeable, historical facts of what happened to your grandmother, but changing the hold those facts have on you. For instance, Maria's dehumanizing legacy was one of terror and silence. Your role in the family line is to break that silence, to name what hides, and thus free yourself and even the memory of your grandmother from it."

"I would like that," Hannah said with quiet determination. "I've felt destined or doomed to carry her silence. But if I can turn it into a story with an ending that offers a sensible conclusion, that would feel like turning doom into, um, I don't know, creation."

"That's a beautiful way to put it," Dr. Jo reacted, smiling warmly, her eyes glistening. "We learn from difficult experiences and pay them forward by doing something good or productive with them. We refer to this as sublimation, a mature and healthy psychological coping mechanism. Moreover, we constantly update our story to meet the circumstances and context of our lives. Turning doom into creation. That could be a line in your article or book someday," Dr. Jo added.

Hannah paused. "It wasn't the same wording, but the feeling was identical. That pressure in the chest. The urgency. The helplessness. I've never read anything that matched my dream like that."

"That sounds very intense. How long have you had this nightmare?" Dr. Jo asked.

"On and off for years," Hannah responded, "But the dream has become more frequent in the past few weeks."

"Since you started working on your fresh writing project, perhaps?" Dr. Jo asked, her brow knitted, revealing and expressing concern. "Sometimes, feelings travel across generations. Not as memories, exactly, but as emotional imprints. What you experienced may be a kind of unconscious echo, your mind's attempt to make sense of something too big, too buried, to hold in words."

"But how?" Hannah queried. "How could I dream of something that happened before I was born to someone I had never met?"

"We know that trauma leaves traces in families and biology. Research has shown that extreme stress can alter gene expression. These changes can affect behavior and emotional reactivity in the next generation."

Hannah looked down at her hands. "It doesn't feel like science. It feels like haunting."

"It can feel that way," Dr. Jo said. "But you're not haunted. You're connected. And your dream isn't a message from the past; it's your psyche reaching for meaning. Trying to tell a story with the fragments it holds."

Hannah's voice quieted, "Maria had a daughter named Ella. Ella was my birth mother."

Dr. Jo's gentle gaze met Hannah's when she looked up. "That's a lot to carry," Dr. Jo whispered.

"I didn't know any of it growing up," Hannah cried. "And now it's like the pieces are rearranging inside me. The stories I told myself about who I am no longer fit."

Dr. Jo nodded again. "That's often what happens when buried truths rise. We call it disorganization, but it's also a form of clarity when what was unspeakable starts to find words."

Hannah looked up. "It's hard to believe that any of this belongs to me," she said innocently.

"But it does," Dr. Jo said. "And the more you can name and meld your feelings with words and visual memory, the less power there is to trigger and disrupt you in the shadows. You are not claiming someone else's pain but acknowledging its legacy. That's different."

"It still hurts," Hannah whispered. "Even if I never lived it."

"Of course it does," Dr. Jo said empathetically as she leaned forward slightly. "You know," she said, "when the nervous system gets overloaded, it helps to return to the five senses. It's not magic; it's just physiology. In trauma therapy, we employ a technique to help patients return to the present moment and dissociate intense, unmanageable emotions from the visual memory of the event. This is achieved by introducing the person to a separate set of stimuli."

She demonstrated with her fingers. "Try this sometime when you're anxious, like you might panic. Look around and name five things you can see. Four things you can touch. Three things you can hear. Two things you can smell. One thing you can taste. It's called 5–4–3–2–1 grounding. This is just a way to anchor your mind in the present." Hannah had not realized how often her body braced for impact, even when nothing was happening.

"Panic attacks can make us feel like we are right back in a traumatic moment, even if it's not our memory," said the doctor. "Your body's alarm system is going haywire, interpreting an old or inherited memory as a current threat. One technique we can try with dreams or experiences during the daytime is to consciously re-enter the dream, flashback, or memory, whatever it might be. At the same time, you're awake and give it a different outcome, or at least stand differently within it."

Hannah wiped away her tears and listened attentively. "Like a guided imagery thing? I might try that," she said with a hint of skepticism.

"Precisely," said Dr. Jo. "You'd close your eyes and visualize the nightmare scene, but with me here guiding you, reminding you you're safe. Would you like to try it? There are no side effects; nothing bad can happen." Hannah nodded.

"All right. Let's make you comfortable first. You could lie back on the couch. Here is an extra pillow. And the blanket is there. Close your eyes when you're ready. Focus on your breath first, inhaling slowly in and out. That's good. You're safe here. I'm right here. Now, I want you to imagine you're in that house from your dream. The one that's like your childhood home but empty. You're in the hallway. Can you see it?"

Hannah closed her eyes. She spoke softly. "Yes, wooden floors, the rug, wallpaper with tiny blue flowers. It's just like our old house, but there is no furniture. And it's cold."

Dr. Jo continued. "You notice it's cold. You're aware of all these details. That's good. Now, you hear it—the crying. The baby was crying behind the walls. The sound is faint, but there. What are you feeling right now?"

Hannah's voice quivered, her body trembling. "I feel panic. I want to get to the baby. I feel desperate."

Dr. Jo pressed on. "OK. That's the familiar part. Now, Hannah, I will ask you to do something in this dream, this image. First, notice yourself. Are you an adult in the dream or a child?"

"I think I'm an adult. Yes, I feel like me now," Hannah said definitively.

"Good. So adult Hannah is in that house. You hear the baby. The walls are there. Now, I want you to imagine someone is there with you."

Hannah says, "I see my mom, Addie, with me." Hannah's hands clench slightly as if grabbing at something. "I am grasping at the door handles, trying to get closer to the screaming, and realize the baby is downstairs in the basement or underground. We get closer to the wailing baby until we finally see her in the cellar, wrapped up in a cloth, her little face red from screaming. I lift her with Mom next to me, and we bundle her. We take her upstairs and start feeding her. She stops crying. She's alive and well."

Dr. Jo exclaimed, "Yes! You saved her! It's safe now, with you and Gran. You both did it together. How do you feel in this moment in the dream?"

"I feel relief. Immense relief," Hannah said, smiling through tears. "And love. So much love is pouring out to this little one. Mom is kissing the baby's head, and I hold them both."

Dr. Jo advised, "Stay in that feeling as long as you want. Let it soak in. Take a few deep breaths. This is a good moment to add yourself as a baby to the visualization. Imagine yourself in the orphanage, and now you're taking care of yourself, too. When you're ready, you can say goodbye to the baby, take it with you, or whatever feels right, and then open your eyes."

"Whoa, that was intense, but I feel lighter, " Hannah said incredulously. "I've cried about this nightmare before, but it always ended with panic. This time, it ended with relief!"

Dr. Jo suggested Hannah consider writing this visualization down as a short story or scene while it was fresh. "The description could be a beautiful piece of your creative project."

Hannah said she would implement the suggestion before sleeping that night. "It will be interesting to see if the nightmare returns, and if it does, would it be a variation or altogether different?

Dr. Jo said, "If it does come, remember, you can change it, even mid-dream now. Sometimes, once you've reimagined it in waking life, the dream shifts or stops recurring. If you have it and wake up, try to recall this moment, and bring back that feeling of relief. That's the power of re-authoring the narrative, even in a visualization. We didn't change the historical truth—tragically, that baby did die—but we gave your psyche a chance to imagine a healing scenario. Such imaginings can help the brain reconcile and let go, knowing that you, as an individual, have faced the fear and transformed it in some way."

Hannah sat up slowly, wiping tears. "It felt like healing in real-time. I could feel the relief in my body—I could breathe much more freely. It brought me true relief, saving that baby. It's uncanny!"

"Empathy is painful," Dr. Jo said. "But it's also the beginning of integration, a prerequisite to loving oneself, equanimity, connection to others, and loving-kindness." Hannah was staggered by Dr. Jo's wisdom.

"Once again, Hannah, it's time for us to stop for today. It was great having this conversation with you. I hope you're pleased and have a good few weeks ahead."

"I will. You, too. Thank you for everything," Hannah said with genuine sincerity.

As she walked out into the evening air, Hannah felt the cool breeze on her face, aware that she was breathing freely for the first time in a long while. The streetlights seemed a little brighter, the world a little more vivid. She was on her way to healing, and she knew it. Although Hannah loved the fact that she was feeling better and deriving tremendous benefit from her work with Dr. Jo, she was anxious about how to include it in the article. *How self-disclosing should I be?* On the one hand, her own experience was organic and palpable. It was more engaging than a clinical, cut-and-dried article. She made a mental note to balance the personal and the factual.

Dr. Jo returned to her study, reflecting on the profound session and silently thanking Hannah for trusting her with such sacred emotional work. Both felt fulfilled and hopeful about their upcoming scheduled conversation.

Chapter 11: Unraveling Threads

The following morning, Hannah sat at her desk, the city's street noise distracting her. Her recorder and notepad lay before her, reminders of the interview with Dr. Brightman. The conversation had been enlightening, but it also stirred questions that lingered in her mind.

Determined to delve deeper into intergenerational trauma, Hannah continued her research. She was a hard worker who could burn the midnight oil and work 18 hours, sometimes even forgetting to eat. Hannah pored over articles, studies, and personal narratives, each explaining how the effects of trauma pass down through generations, not just through stories but embedded in DNA, behaviors, and unspoken fears. She constructed a list of important interview questions, allowing Dr. Jo to unfold her story engagingly and naturally.

One story stood out, of a woman who discovered that her chronic anxiety mirrored that of her grandmother, a Holocaust survivor. Despite being generations apart and having never discussed such feelings, the reiterations of past traumas resonated within her.

Reflecting on her own life, Hannah couldn't help but draw parallels. She thought of her adoptive mother, Addie, and her mother, Hannah's grandmother, Gran, whose superstitions, rituals, and anxieties had shaped Hannah's upbringing. While Addie's practices seemed eccentric, they were rooted in a deep-seated need for protection, stemming from her hidden wounds.

The image of her birth mother, Ella, surfaced in her mind. The photograph she had found years ago depicted a woman with eyes that held stories untold. What fears and experiences had Ella faced? And how much of that was now a part of Hannah?

Hannah realized that understanding Dr. Brightman's work wasn't merely about drafting an article, but a personal journey into her own history. By unraveling the threads of the past interwoven with the present, she could find clarity and healing. She recognized that the mind is a tangled spool; one tug and the pattern shifted. Hannah felt as if a window inside her had opened, letting in memories that she wasn't ready to confront.

Dr. Jo's name had surfaced in three conversations before the assignment landed. Once at a dinner party; once at her therapist's office, who said, "You might like her work—it's rigorous but deeply human"; and then again, in a podcast episode Hannah had played randomly one night when she couldn't sleep. Each time, it felt like someone was nudging her, like the universe had a foot pressed gently against her back.

Hannah worried that she sounded like her mother now, doing the same thing cognitively—a flaky way of attributing causality to unrelated events and circumstances. She had conjured up the story about the chest being an omen because her mother conflated serial events with the words *Entre Nous*, deciding that the chest was a sign of grave importance. *So ridiculous.*

With renewed determination, Hannah outlined her next steps: Two more interviews with Dr. Brightman; connecting with individuals who had experienced inherited trauma; and confronting her own past more directly. She tried to understand what pulled her toward this assignment. Trauma was a word she had used sparingly, even regarding her own. Sure, her adoptive mom had her quirks—warped silence around her childhood, and an iron will. Still, Hannah had grown up in the suburbs, not in a war zone. She'd had tooth braces. And work deadlines. Nothing unmanageable or terrible.

Still, something stirred in her when she read Dr. Jo's book. She realized she was interested in what we inherit from the untold stories. She needed to find out what filled the void. So, her path ahead was uncertain, but she was ready to navigate it.

The following week, while walking through Central Park with her friend Lucy, they sat on a bench to take a break. Hannah noticed an older woman next to her with a numbered tattoo on her arm. She began to feel a tightness in her chest, as if the air was hard to inhale. She paused to focus on her breath and quietly did the 5–4–3–2–1 grounding exercise Dr. Jo taught her. *Five things I see: the curve of the path, a stroller, someone's blue shoelaces, a yellow leaf, and Lucy. I feel four things: my scarf against my neck, the wooden bench, the ground under my feet, and how I'm clenching my jaw. Three things I hear: birds chirping, a child laughing, and a honking horn. Two things I smell: the damp earth, and a hint of coffee. One thing I taste: the mint from the gum I've been chewing.* Little by little, her body began to remember that it was safe.

Hannah glanced at Lucy and smiled sheepishly, hoping she had not noticed her inner workings. "Sorry, I just needed a moment to reset."

Lucy put her arm around Hannah and reminded her there was no need to apologize. She was impressed at how quickly she dealt with the anxiety. At that moment, Hannah realized that she needed to have compassion for herself. She understood what triggered her and managed her emotions. This feeling of agency was new.

Chapter 12: Grounded

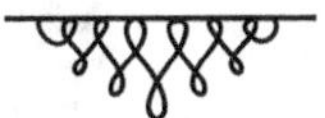

Dr. Josephine Brightman sat in her usual chair, one leg crossed over the other, glasses resting low on her nose. Hannah had begun to think of this room as something between a sanctuary and a forge. She entered heavy and unsure; she left lighter and clearer, at least for now.

"You look different today," Dr. Jo said, setting her tea aside.

Hannah felt a flutter of anticipation. "Yeah, I feel stronger. I feel different," she admitted. "Like something is taking shape. Not finished, but forming. I haven't had a panic attack in the last two weeks. Not even once. I came close several times, but I used the techniques we discussed. I even did that grounding thing in the frozen foods aisle at the grocery store when I felt one creeping in out of nowhere. I must've looked ridiculous, muttering, 'Five oranges, four cereal boxes, three people, two cartwheels, one freezer door handle,' but it worked."

Dr. Jo and Hannah both laughed. "That's fantastic," Dr. Jo regaled. "And not silly, or even if it was, who cares? It kept you present."

"Yup. Exactly. Hannah added. "And guess what? No more nightmares of the baby in the cellar! Not once since our last meeting."

Dr. Jo blasted out some comments and questions: "That's huge. How do you feel about that? Any part of you strangely misses it, or is it just relief?"

Hannah considered. "Hmm. It's a relief, mostly. But interestingly, I had another dream. It wasn't a nightmare; it wasn't a disturbing dream at all. So, I dreamed I was walking through the village where Gran grew up. It was quiet and peaceful. I saw a little girl who I knew was Gran, and she waved at me. And I waved back. That was it. I woke up feeling content."

"That gave me goosebumps," Dr. Jo said. "It's like your mind created a new closing scene for that chapter—a peaceful one. Terrific. In that vein, let's focus our conversation today on reflective insight and narrative integration. So, we can discuss how you're integrating all these experiences into your story of yourself and your identity moving forward."

Hannah opened her notebook. The pages were filled with sketches, quotes, and phrases circled in red. She was no longer scribbling to chase clarity—now, she was mapping it. A little time pressure weighed on her: She was already six weeks into her article, and even without a hard deadline, she was planning on going to London soon and needed to work on it more assiduously.

"I've been thinking about those AMCs you mentioned," she began. "They're like default settings, right? Formed in childhood?"

Dr. Jo nodded. "They're not just habits of thought; they're whole belief systems shaped by the child's most important relationships, which are internalized, child and parent style of attachment, traumas, temperament, and inherited emotional memory. Most of them operate unconsciously. 95% of our mental activity happens outside our awareness. Look over Chapter 4 of *Yesterday Never Rests* for a discussion of unconscious motivation, AMCs, and the iceberg metaphor."

"That's what I keep circling," Hannah said. "It's like I am not just reacting to the present but playing out old compromises."

Dr. Jo's eyes brightened. "Exactly. In psychoanalytic terms, those compromises are what Freud called compromise formations—the psyche's way of negotiating among competing internal forces. It's a way of settling internal conflict. For example, according to Freud, anxiety, dreams, fantasies, and various aspects of the character result from 'compromise formations': a truce between a forbidden wish and the mind's resistance to acting upon that wish. I find the term quite useful. It effectively describes how the mind's warring factions work together by negotiating and accepting that compromise which is often the best outcome in resolving inner conflicts. The id wants one thing, the critical and perfectionistic superego another. The ego does what it can to achieve inner peace—a healthy outcome. My AMCs are a modern version of that model. They reflect how the mind organizes itself to survive, not always to thrive. The result may manifest as a symptom of a very pathological condition, or it might instead be an adaptive, healthy trait or attitude seen as normal behavior."

"So, an embattled mind is in a constant state of tug of war," Hannah stated. "It must be exhausting, like running a program in the background that drains all your battery."

"Good conceptualization. This is why self-reflection is the key to mental health. I use this metaphor with patients: the unconscious mind is like a blind spot in the rearview mirror. You can't see or know what's shaping your reactions, but it's at the periphery of consciousness. Sometimes, you're more aware of it than others. You can be in danger of an accident until you learn to check for it deliberately."

"Is that what therapy is? Learning to check your blind spot?" Hannah asked.

"Yes. And eventually learning to update your navigation system, not just avoid collisions."

Hannah smiled at that. "And the unconscious? That's the driver we're not even aware is steering half the time?"

"Freud describes the mind as an iceberg, with most hidden beneath the surface. When we see 'the tip of the iceberg,' that's our conscious mind. Everything that is submerged is the unconscious. Our motives, memories, and conflicts lie within us. Just because we can't see the bulk of the iceberg doesn't mean it's not directing us."

"And AMCs live down there?" Hannah asked.

"Right. They're internalized from our earliest interactions, especially through attachment relationships. And trauma can distort the messages so deeply that the body takes over where the words failed." Dr. Jo paused, then added, "There's also a physiological cost to this chronic stress. People with inherited trauma often have depleted cortisol reserves, and impaired immune responses. Their systems become less effective. Consequently, it becomes more challenging to fight off infection, chronic illness, and cancer."

Hannah looked down. "So, this isn't just psychological. It's cellular."

"Yes. And naming it doesn't make it go away—but it gives you agency. It puts your hands on the wheel again."

"That makes sense," Hannah said. "I feel like I've been in a knot my whole life. Lately, things are loosening. Not unwinding, just softening."

"The goal isn't to undo the knot," said Dr. Jo. "It's to understand what it holds together."

Hannah sat with that. She jotted it down in her notebook, adding a star in the margin. "Yes. The body remembers, even when the mind can't find a reason."

"Hannah, the past doesn't sleep. It waits until we are still enough to hear it. And if it's essential, it will keep coming back. We don't need to go looking for it. Not to beat a dead horse or be overly academic, but I think it's important to know the four different epigenetic pathways through which the stress effects of trauma can be transmitted. Interrupt me if I start lecturing. I sometimes get carried away when talking about this topic."

"By all means."

"OK. The first is relational, as evidenced by caregiving behavior, which has observable effects and is the focus of my work and that of many psychoanalytic therapists. The direct impact of your grandmother's silence on you emotionally is illustrative of the direct effect. For example, the way I hated lamb before ever seeing, smelling, or tasting it because my mother was disgusted by it."

"Second, the effects can be passed down culturally, such as embedded beliefs about racism and antisemitism, historical trauma, or events like slavery or the Holocaust."

"Third, traumatic effects can be passed down as secondary trauma—things we hear and see. For example, people who witnessed a murder may have PTSD, as might people who watched the World Trade Center come down on 9/11 or repeated television and online viewings of casualties and murders." Hannah nodded, remembering.

"Lastly, ITT—intergenerational transmission of trauma's effects through generations—can be transmitted epigenetically through the DNA, through the germ cell, mitosis, and even via the placenta and birth canal. I just wanted to give you an idea so you can research it further, but it's beyond our scope today."

The doctor continued. "To illustrate, consider a mind-blowing case—I believe you brought it up when we first met. So, I am referring to fundamental biology. Recall the well-known study we spoke about; the mice conditioned to fear the specific smell of cherry blossoms, and their pups who were afraid of that smell, even though they'd never encountered it with their senses. Now, consider that pregnant women who were in their second or third trimester who endured 9/11, for instance, might pass a heightened stress response to their children. Or a father who survived a war might unknowingly program his kid to be on alert. Not in a deterministic, one-for-one way as there are plenty of factors that shape a child—but there's a carryover. Think of it as an echo of trauma. The original sound is the parent's experience, and the echo is a faint but present effect in the child's body and subconscious. They might have higher baseline anxiety, or be easily startled, or struggle with trust without knowing why."

An echo of trauma. Hannah tensed up around an old ache. She had been adopted as an infant, she had no idea what fears or sorrows her birth mother, Ella, carried in her heart while pregnant with her. Hannah only knew that she had battled anxiety since childhood; free-floating worry that never quite made sense. As a little girl, she'd had nightmares of being abandoned, though her adoptive parents were nothing but loving. *Where did such nightmares come from? Perhaps some invisible hand-me-down of Ella's fears.* The thought was at once eerie and oddly comforting. Hannah was not crazy; she was connected in ways she was beginning to understand. She didn't want to bring this stuff up again with Dr. Jo. *Relax,* she thought to herself. *I am conducting an interview series, not engaging in personal therapy sessions.*

Her gaze focused, Dr. Jo continued, "Let's return to the study with the mice I mentioned a few minutes ago."

"That is uncanny," Hannah retorted with confidence. "Since mice and humans share 95% of DNA, it's simple to extrapolate and assume that the same happens to humans."

"Correct. It's hard to prove with humans because we need multigenerational studies, and we can't lock people up in a lab for generations."

Both women laughed and enjoyed their conversation. Hannah was thrilled to learn from Dr. Jo.

She had a question that she worried was off-topic. "Dr. Jo…why do you do this kind of work? Specifically, inherited trauma?"

Dr. Jo needed a moment to gather her thoughts. "Because it found me before I saw it. I grew up in a house where silence did the talking. Grief was in the wallpaper, in the air. And no one named it. When I studied neuroscience and psychoanalysis, I realized the legacy wasn't just emotional but structural. Cellular. And I wanted to give it language. Because once we name something and meld language, visual memory, and words, it loses its hold over us."

Hannah sat with that wise comment. She jotted it down in her notebook, again adding a star in the margin.

"And I've been thinking a lot about Maria, my grandmother, and her Yellow Diary. Her silence wasn't just survival. It became an inheritance. And Ella, too. Her absence taught me something about abandonment long before I had words for it."

Dr. Jo leaned forward. "And Addie?" she asked.

Hannah was quiet. "She tried. I know that now. She gave me safety, but not always resonance. Sometimes she didn't get it. She wanted to protect me from my past by pretending it didn't matter. But it did."

Dr. Jo nodded. "Safety without recognition can feel like dismissal. Even when it's offered with love."

Hannah exhaled. In silence, she thought, *That's what I wrote this morning: love without acknowledgment can feel like erasure.* Hannah had an epiphany. She finally understood her anger toward her mother, Addie. It was her lack of acknowledging that Ella was only her birth mother, but Addie was her actual, excellent mother; having parents who loved her was not second-rate. For the first time in her life, Hannah felt sorry for making Addie the butt of her unresolved anger and hurt feelings about the adoption. She still intended to find her birth mother someday, but there was no rush. *I mean, it's cool—I'm glad that Ella loved me, but, honestly, what good did it do for me?* Now was not the time. It was time to reconcile with the woman who had raised and loved her from the start.

Hannah said, "I wrote something just like that statement this morning. You say safety without recognition can feel like dismissal, and I wrote that love without acknowledgment can feel like erasure."

Dr. Jo added, "You're writing again."

"Yes. I've started the article for *Currents*." Hannah opened the notebook. Pages fluttered with arrows and scribbles. She hesitated for a moment. Was this too personal? Was she crossing some line between subject and writer, or is that boundary already long gone? She decided to trust the process and carried on. She read aloud: "What if our ancestors don't haunt us in dreams, but in patterns? In the clench of a jaw, the urge to run, the startle at sirens. What if grief is a blueprint passed down, remodeled, but never quite demolished?"

Hannah looked up. "Too much?"

Dr. Jo smiled. "It's not too much. It's the truth, finally told in your voice."

They sat quietly for a moment. Hannah could feel the article taking shape, not as a profile of a professional, but as a portrait of a process—of unraveling and remembering, of becoming the author of her mind.

She sat back with her notebook now closed. "Wow, I see that I am not just drafting this article. I'm rewriting my life. And I think I'm ready to live it."

Chapter 13: Storytelling

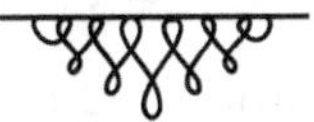

For their final interview, Hannah and Dr. Jo agreed to discuss the article, the personal narrative, and the importance of storytelling. After settling into their chairs, Dr. Jo said, "You know, Hannah, one of the core ideas in my work is the power of story—what we call narrative identity. Have you come across that term?"

Hannah nodded. "The idea that we shape our identity by the stories we tell about ourselves, right? Changing that story can change how we see ourselves. When I was younger, one therapist taught me to name what I was feeling like an outside commentator: my heart is racing; my body thinks it's in danger, but I notice I'm safe. It helped. I thought of it as stepping outside the panic for a second.

"Exactly. Each time you do that—each time you recognize an automatic pattern or inherited fear—you lay a tiny new pathway. You prove to yourself you're not completely controlled by it. Multiply those moments over time, and the new pathway can become dominant. The old construct may never vanish, but it can diminish—like a roaring river turned into a brook. Humans are storytelling creatures at our core. We make meaning out of our lives by stringing events into narratives: 'This happened; therefore, I am this kind of person, and thus my life will go in that direction.' Trauma disrupts that narrative, like someone tearing out or blacking out key pages of our book."

Dr. Jo's voice took on a lyrical cadence, and Hannah realized this must be a subject the psychoanalyst was passionate about. "When something shatters your life—say, a sudden death, or a childhood of abuse, or being uprooted from your home—you don't just lose a person or a place. You lose the story of who you thought you were. The plot no longer makes sense. Why did this happen? What does it mean for me? Who am I now?"

Hannah felt a pang of recognition. When David died so suddenly, she had felt exactly that way: as if the entire future story she'd imagined was erased, leaving her staring at a blank, meaningless page. And being adopted, too, had always given her a sense of missing the beginning of her own story. She often felt like a book started halfway through, always guessing at what came before. Relief and hope warred with her usual cynicism. Could she really change the deep grooves in her psyche? It sounded too good to be true. But here she was—proof that change was possible. She was confronting her past, having this conversation, even feeling optimistic.

Dr. Jo went on, her hands expressive as she painted the idea. "Healing often comes through re-storying our lives and telling the tale fully—beginning, middle, and an unfinished end. Even the act of you researching your biological family, reading old letters or diaries, is you gathering the missing chapters of your narrative. And, in time, you'll integrate them into a new understanding of yourself."

Hannah's eyes widened. She hadn't told Dr. Jo about the letters yet—she had barely mentioned the family story beyond being adopted. "How did you—" she began, then smiled, answering her question. "Of course. That's what I've been doing, isn't it? I have some letters my birth mother wrote. I only recently found them. I haven't dared to read them all yet." Her voice quavered with that admission. She hadn't said it out loud before.

Dr. Jo spoke compassionately. "Take your time," she said softly. "Those letters have been patient for years; they will wait until you are ready. But know that when you read them, you engage in one of the most profound healing acts: bearing witness to your own story." She gave Hannah a small, reassuring smile. "Sometimes the story is all we have. And it can be enough."

Hannah realized she was gripping the arm of her chair tightly. She released it and flexed her fingers. "This is going to sound strange," she said, "but I feel like…like I'm here for more than an article. Like life brought me here for a reason." She shook her head, embarrassed by her earnestness. "Sorry, I promise I'm not usually so woo-woo. My parents have a thing about *bashert*, the Yiddish word for destiny. The concept has rubbed off on me."

Dr. Jo's laugh was a soft chiming. "No apology needed. I don't think it's woo-woo or flaky at all. We can call it serendipity or openness. You were ready to find meaning in this assignment, and so you are. And I'm glad."

"Me too," Hannah admitted, tucking a lock of hair behind her ear. She felt a surprising kinship with this woman she'd only just met, which was unexpected and disorienting. But not unpleasant.

She glanced at her notebook, noticing how many prepared questions she hadn't needed to ask outright; the conversation had naturally flowed over them. One remained that she still wanted to cover, one more bit of "science" to round out Dr. Jo's picture.

"May I ask one more thing?" Hannah said as she flipped through her notes. There were still so many threads. She wondered how on earth she would structure this article. Could she even write this without becoming part of the story? She didn't think so at this point.

"It's about change. Everything we've talked about—these ingrained patterns, these repetitions of trauma, the way the brain keeps us on guard—can sound a bit fatalistic. Like we're stuck with the sins of the past. But I get the sense you don't believe people are stuck. You mentioned awareness as a key. What about the idea of neuroplasticity? I know that term vaguely—the brain's ability to change itself."

Dr. Jo's expression brightened, and she nodded. "I'm so glad you brought that up. Yes, neuroplasticity is a beacon of hope in all this. It refers to the brain's malleability and capacity to form new connections and pathways throughout life. It's strongest when we're young, but we know it never stops. Even an old brain can learn new tricks, given the right conditions."

"So even if someone has inherited heightened anxiety or developed an AMC in childhood, they can rewire that?" Hannah asked.

"To a significant degree, yes," Dr. Jo said. "But it's not as simple as flipping a switch. It often requires consistent experiences or practices that gently nudge the brain toward a new way of being. Therapy can do that. Similarly, mindfulness practices, healthy relationships, and creative endeavors like writing or art can also be beneficial. Anything that helps someone experience a new pattern repeatedly can start carving a new neural pathway." Dr. Jo continued, saying that the same principles applied to physiological processes and changes, such as a person eating carefully to lower cholesterol and prevent diabetes. "Mind and body are pliable and malleable; they work together in concert."

Dr. Jo leaned forward a bit, her tone earnest. "One thing I emphasize is cultivating an 'observing self.' It's a slightly technical term, but the idea is simple: it's the part of you that can watch your thoughts and feelings with a bit of distance. Like stepping outside yourself for a moment. When you feel a wave of anxiety, instead of just being anxious, conjure your observing self, and note, 'Ah, I'm feeling anxiety because my old fear of abandonment is triggered.' That act of observing changes what happens in the brain. You move from the automatic part of the cycle into a conscious space. It's like pausing on a movie— suddenly you can see the scene rather than being swept up in it."

Hannah found herself nodding vigorously. "I think I know what you mean. I mentioned I had a therapist when I was younger who taught me to be more introspective and to watch my emotions. She helped me calm my triggers—to observe myself instead of freaking out."

"That's exactly it," said Dr. Jo, clearly pleased. "That's the observing self in action. And each time you do that—each time you recognize an automatic pattern or a surge of inherited fear for what it is—you lay down a tiny new pathway in your mind. You prove to yourself, at least for a moment, that the pattern does not completely control you. Multiply those moments over time, and the new pathway can become dominant. The old automatic construct might never disappear entirely. Remember, trauma leaves marks that can diminish, like a once roaring river now just a babbling brook. I believe the best habit a person can cultivate is to develop a strong observing self. The best way to harness intense emotion is to stand away for a moment and observe."

Hannah let out a breath she had not realized she was holding. Here she was, living proof that some change was possible: she was confronting her past, engaging in this conversation, and even feeling optimistic. When was the last time she had felt that?

She smiled a genuine, buoyant smile. "You make it sound doable. Hard, but doable."

Dr. Jo mirrored the smile. "It is hard, but yes, doable. Humans have an immense ability to heal. I've seen clients transform their lives in ways that, if I had not seen firsthand, I'd hardly believe. Often, it begins with something as simple as telling the truth about what happened and realizing it is not the whole of who they are. Realizing they can shape what happens next."

Hannah felt a deep resonance with those words. Telling the truth about what happened. She thought of the letters in the "Ella" shoebox waiting in her closet. She thought of her half-written files on her laptop, where she'd tried to write about losing David but always stopped short. She had been trying to heal on her own, in fits and starts, through writing—and now life had handed her a guide in the form of Dr. Jo. Serendipity indeed.

The late afternoon light had shifted away from the window; Hannah realized with a start that they had been talking for an hour. She hadn't touched her notebook in a while; the conversation had long since flowed freely beyond her scripted questions. She glanced at the recorder—yes, still running. Good. This was gold, both professionally and personally.

Dr. Jo noticed her glance and softly said, "We've covered a lot, haven't we?"

Hannah laughed. "We have. I can't believe time's almost up." She truly felt that—she could have sat here for hours more, delving into each tendril of thought. Her initial nerves were a distant memory; in their place was a kind of kindled excitement and a strange comfort, as if some heavy weight had started to lift off her without her even noticing.

"I don't want to keep you longer than you planned," Hannah said, reluctant though she was to leave. She stopped the recorder and tucked it into her bag. "I'll need to transcribe all this and digest it. You have given me so much to think about."

"I'm glad," Dr. Jo said. "I've enjoyed this too, Hannah. Talking with someone who genuinely wants to understand is energizing. And hearing a bit of your story has been a privilege."

"Thank you," she said earnestly, meeting Dr. Jo's eyes. "Not just for your time, but for how open you've been. This time with you has been among the most insightful and engaging conversations I've ever had." She stopped, glancing up at Dr. Jo a little shyly.

Dr. Jo smiled and nodded. "I'm glad to hear that. So, what about the concept of narrative integration? How do you see your 'story' now versus when we first met?"

Hannah paused to reflect. "Eight weeks ago, my story was like a collection of fragments I wasn't sure how to assemble. I had a successful young journalist, Hannah, on the one hand, doing fine in her career, etc., and then an anxious, haunted Hannah on the other, dealing with panic and blocks. And the two Hannahs felt at odds, like one of them was a fraud. I was either faking being OK or not being OK—if that makes sense."

"It does seem like an internal inconsistency in your self-narrative," Dr. Jo replied. "I believe recognizing these opposing self-views, working out their internal inconsistencies, and making them compatible is the cornerstone of gaining resilience."

"Yes. Now, I feel like a more integrated person," Hannah said, quickly realizing that sounded too inflated. "I mean…I am a successful young writer, and I also have anxiety stemming from deep, meaningful places. Both are true. Neither makes the other untrue. They inform each other. My sensitivity, which can manifest as anxiety, also fuels my empathy and creativity. It's two sides of the same coin."

Dr. Jo snapped her fingers in agreement. "Yup. Our greatest strengths are our most significant vulnerabilities. You feel panic strongly because you feel everything intensely. And that is a gift when channeled into writing or connection."

"I'm starting to appreciate that," Hannah said. "I hated that sensitive part of me that couldn't handle my life like I thought everyone else could. Now I realize many people are quietly faking it or privately dealing with their stuff. And I'm not broken for having these feelings. If anything, I was breaking down by not allowing myself to acknowledge them."

"There's a term in psychology: post-traumatic growth," Dr. Jo added. "It's when people come out of struggles or therapy with more strength, insight, or resilience than before—because of the battle, not despite it. You've experienced some of that."

Hannah brightened and animatedly said, "Definitely. Facing this has made me more resilient. It's almost paradoxical. I've become stronger by allowing myself to be vulnerable and sometimes feel broken."

Dr. Jo tried to ignore a subliminal worry that her husband would be upset. She would be 15 minutes late for their dinner with friends. Even though it was time for her to terminate this interview, she was on a roll, and this was, after all, her first interview for a major lay publication, on a par with *The Atlantic* or *Vanity Fair*. Reorienting herself to the present moment, she said, "Paradox is often the name of the game in healing. Another concept comes to mind: 'turning ghosts into ancestors.' It's an idea from family therapy. The ghosts are those unspoken, unresolved issues in a family, like Maria's traumatic experiences, which are lurking in your life. When you face and integrate them, they become ancestral, acknowledged parts of your history that you can draw strength from rather than just being haunted by them."

Hannah's eyes widened. "I love that!" Hannah exclaimed. "Ghosts into ancestors. That's precisely what happened. The crying baby, the trauma—that story was a menacing ghost. Now, it's more like an ancestor, a story I've inherited that I can learn from and carry without fear but with respect, because it doesn't spook me anymore. I have an organic understanding of the therapeutic power of naming and constructing a personal story.

"I think I have a framework now," Hannah continued. "Instead of seeing a panic attack as this awful, random curse, I can say, OK, here's anxiety, triggered by X, it's telling a story about Y. I can even personify it, like we joked, and deal with it as part of my story, not as an enemy. And don't get me wrong, but I see no glory in suffering. I loved Prozac. It got rid of my panic attacks 100%, but I had such harmful side effects that I had to stop taking it. Nothing wrong with good psychopharmacology."

"Yes," Dr. Jo responded, "I agree that there's no glory in suffering, and we need to do whatever we can for ourselves. I see how you've developed a narrative language for your experiences. You gave them characters and a plot. That's so helpful in robbing them of their mystery and menace."

"And I'm sure I'll still have moments. But I don't anticipate them with dread as much," Hannah added. "I have many positive experiences to draw on: our conversations, my writing about them, and even that visualization exercise. They're like touchstones I can revisit. I may need one mental toolbox on this big trip I am about to take to London."

"That's wonderful. And what about your trip? I don't believe you mentioned that you were going traveling overseas," said Dr. Jo, visibly surprised.

Hannah, grinned. "I'm excited. I think I'm a little anxious, but it's normal anxiety. It's a big trip, and I'll be researching my ancestry. I expect it will be emotionally heavy when I'm there. There is also a love interest there, a man that I've fallen for. It feels like he may be the one."

"Hannah, this seems like a fascinating time in your life. You might find more puzzle pieces and new stories to add while there. I hope you enjoy London. I wish you the absolute best with your love Interest. I hope everything goes your way."

"Absolutely. I plan to. Dr. Jo, I also wanted to say that even though we called this an interview series, it has been very therapeutic for me. Although I plan to draft the article for *Currents* to publish, these six hours with you have been life-changing for me, a real game changer."

Dr. Jo reached over to touch Hannah's hand gently. "That is the best outcome I could hope for. And if you write about it, in whatever form, it will resonate with many because you write about humanity at its core—history, family, emotions, all from an organic place. A bit of humor and warmth also goes a long way in building trust and safety."

Hannah's eyes started to well up, but this time with gratitude, not pain. "Having a real, organic, in-the-lab kind of experience that was genuine and not contrived will drive the article. It is easy for me to be open. I'm so grateful," she said, wiping her eyes. "Yet I am also sad this is ending. But it's a good kind of sad, like finishing a terrific book."

Dr. Jo beamed. "That is high praise, being compared to a terrific book experience. But remember, our conversations don't have to end forever. We can always check in with a follow-up conversation when you return from London," Dr. Jo said reassuringly. "Before we finish, is there anything else on your mind? Do you have any lingering questions, fears, or thoughts you'd like to voice?"

Hesitantly, unsure of how to articulate her thoughts, Hannah ventured, "Just one thing. Do you think healing provides lasting change? I mean, I feel great now, but I worry. What if, in a year, I'm back to square one? How do I keep this growth going?"

"That's an excellent question," Dr. Jo said. She proceeded with a more serious tone. "Healing isn't usually linear, and it's not a one-time achievement like leveling up in a video game where you never lose that power. Life can throw new challenges, and old feelings might resurface. But, crucially, you're not the same person you were before. You have new tools, insights, and a track record of overcoming. Think of it like you've climbed one mountain, so you know you can climb others. The terrain might differ, and you might need to rest or get a guide again, but you won't be starting from nothing. Square one? I doubt you'll ever be back there. You might feel like you backslide sometimes, but even then, it's usually a spiral staircase—it might feel like you're down, but you're still moving forward, just in a way that revisits themes at a higher level."

Comforted, Hannah said, "I like the spiral staircase metaphor. Even if I come around to the same spot, I'm a level up in understanding. I feel like I have had a good start."

"And don't underestimate the changes that have begun," Dr. Jo added. "You said you feel more integrated now and can't undo what you know about yourself. You might forget or doubt temporarily, but you have a solid foundation to return to."

Dr. Jo's response gave Hannah a sense of security and reassurance. She thought to herself that journaling helps her stay connected with her feelings and visceral responses rather than avoiding them. Seeking therapy if needed would hold her in good stead. It was all about staying aware and compassionate towards oneself.

Hannah sighed contentedly, then became noticeably agitated, startled.

"Oh," she blurted, "I forgot that I wanted to read some skeletal segments of the article. It'll only take a few minutes. Is that OK? Or would you prefer that I email it to you? Or do you want to wait until it's ready to read the published version?" When Hannah felt anxious or out of control around a person, she would often bombard them with questions in this manner. It was as if she had to give someone the full drop-down menu of choices to control their response options.

Dr. Jo smiled fondly at Hannah, awed by how much the young journalist embraced this process. She was aware of Hannah's anxiety, but this wasn't the time to address it.

"Of course, please read it! I wouldn't miss it for the world! My husband will understand if I'm a few minutes late for an important reason," Dr. Jo replied. The message implied that her schedule allowed only a few extra minutes.

Hannah flipped open her notebook. She had arrived prepared for the final interview session, with a nice summary and various parts of the article which were ready. Hannah read the passages she had written:

I began these conversations seeking an interview but found a therapeutic journey. With Josephine Brightman, MD, at my side, gently I excavated years, generations of silence and fear in eight weeks. I named the ghosts of the past: panic, nightmare, the effects of inherited trauma, and creative paralysis. And in naming them, I found they were not demons to slay, but stories to listen to. I learned that the baby in my recurring dream had to finally cry out for me to hear what needed to be heard. I learned that my panic was a messenger, not a madness. I learned that by telling my story, I honor those who came before me and empower those who come after. I stand now, not free of fear but unafraid of feeling it.

Hanna took a sip of water, cleared her throat, and continued:

We inherit more than eye color and temperament. We inherit stories that were never told aloud. Memories that were too painful to name. Those silences are thick enough to shape our lives.

While researching this article, I sat down with Dr. Brightman, a psychoanalyst trained in neuroscience and psychiatry who works at the intersection of trauma psychology, biology, and the unconscious mind. I came to her as a journalist but left changed as a person. What I learned isn't just a theory—it's a mirror that reflects how much of ourselves we don't yet understand.

Dr. Brightman explained that most of us move through the world operating under what she calls AMCs—Automatic Mental Constructs. Our earliest relationships and environments shape these emotional algorithms we create and internalize in childhood. AMCs help us survive, but they also limit our freedom. They are not beliefs we consciously choose. They are compromises within the inner mind seeking a truce and avoiding conflict, shame, and abandonment. Dr. Sigmund Freud called these internal negotiations "compromise formations." In modern language, they are the detours we take around unresolved pain—how we smile when we want to cry, or disconnect emotionally before anyone can leave us. The unconscious doesn't just store memories; it drives behavior. As Freud's famous metaphor shows us, the mind is like an iceberg. Only a small tip is visible above the water. The vast majority—the motivations, fears, and desires—lies beneath.

Neuroscience confirms what Freud intuited over a century ago: that more than 95% of our mental processing occurs unconsciously. Our bodies react before our brains can explain. The child who grew up careful not to provoke, watching his parents, cautiously, becomes the adult who anticipates abandonment, even in safe relationships. That is not a weakness. It is wiring.

What's most astonishing is that trauma doesn't end with the individual; it can also affect their loved ones. Through a process known as epigenetic inheritance, stress responses are passed across a generation and from one generation to the next. A grandchild may have cortisol abnormalities linked not to her suffering but to the grief of a grandmother she never met. Chronic hyper-vigilance, anxiety, apathy, depression, and even autoimmune disorders can have ancestral origins. Our bodies carry the blueprint of memory—personal and collective. And until we examine that blueprint, we are at its mercy.

I used to think healing meant erasing the past. I discovered that healing means integrating, naming, and letting it inform but not define us. We cannot make peace with the world until we make peace with the map we've inherited. That means listening to our thoughts, the tension in our shoulders, the dreams we keep having, and the flinch we can't explain.

It also means learning to befriend the unconscious to become curious about our blind spots, as one might with a rearview mirror. What we don't see can still hit us, but we might change course if we learn to check the angles.

This is not just about mental health. It's about reclaiming authorship. It's about agency. About becoming someone who chooses—not just reacts—who remembers with compassion and moves forward with courage. It is not a betrayal when the body remembers what the mind forgot. It is an invitation to listen, learn, and begin again.

"Hannah, that's beautiful. You captured it so eloquently," Dr. Jo said.

Hannah felt herself blush. "Of course. High praise coming from a writer I admire. Thank you."

"Hannah, the description encapsulates your journey. 'My panic was a messenger, not a madness' is a crucial reframe. Being 'unafraid of feeling fear' is such a powerful concept. Fear is not the enemy; avoidance of fear is the bigger problem. As President Franklin Delano Roosevelt said, 'The only thing we must fear is fear itself.' I don't think anyone can phrase it any better than that."

"Exactly, Hannah said. "I've always tried to avoid fear, which only made it stronger. Now I'm like, 'OK, fear, come along if you must. Just don't drive the car.'"

Dr. Jo loved the imagery. "Fear can sit in the backseat, seatbelt on, quietly observing while you drive."

"Yes, it could even be a backseat driver sometimes, but I can ignore the nagging and the bad advice it yells—turn left because there's danger ahead! No thanks, fear, I got this."

Dr. Jo was impressed with Hannah's great internal dialogue. A bit of sass, sarcasm, and humor gives fear its place and diminishes its hold. "Humor is a mature and valuable coping mechanism," she said.

Hannah couldn't live without it. Despite all the darkness, her family has a wicked sense of humor, including Gran, who could tell a mean joke when she wanted to.

Dr. Jo continued, "It's often a survival tactic too. I recall many stories of Holocaust survivors who credited humor for surviving. Humor can be defiance in the face of despair, a refusal to let the darkness have all the power."

"True," said Hannah pensively. "I think Hannah Glass, the writer, needs to remember that she is the character in her own life story." She stood up, knowing it was time for her to go. Dr. Jo stood up too.

Hannah smiled and said, "Use humor for some levity when things get too heavy."

Dr. Jo was *verklempt*. She dabbed her misty eyes with a tissue; visibly moved and touched. "I will carry your story as a reminder of why I love what I do. I am moved by your words, Hannah. People like you make it worthwhile, and then some."

The two women shared a hug that captured the gratitude and affection that words could not fully achieve. When they stepped back, both took a moment to compose themselves, smiling through glistening tears.

With one last smile, Hannah turned and left the study. Dr. Jo watched her go, feeling a swell of pride and a tinge of that good sadness Hannah mentioned.

Hannah stepped out into the dusk, amazed at how bright the world looked and how steady she felt. She'd be heading to London in a week and into a future she was ready to embrace—ghosts acknowledged, ancestors honored, and her own story to tell.

In the following weeks, Dr. Jo received a postcard from London with a picture of Big Ben. On the back, Hannah had written: "Saw the Thames at sunset. Thought of our chats. No ghosts here, only history and hope. Love, Hannah."

Dr. Jo pinned the card to her office cork board, a reminder of Hannah's journey and the beautiful, ever-evolving conversation between past and present, fear and creativity, healer and healed.

Chapter 14: The Bath

Hannah sank into the steaming water, letting the porcelain tub envelop her body. The bathroom lights were dim, just as she liked—soft amber, like candlelight without the romantic commitment. Steam curled upward from the surface, fogging the mirror above the sink and clouding her thoughts just enough so the neighbor's blaring hard rock music did not disrupt her peaceful moment.

The bath was her ritual, one of the few nice things she did for herself. There she could unwind and unravel the knots of her mind and body without trying too hard. No deadlines. No editor. Just luxuriating in water and revery.

She pressed the soles of her feet against the end of the tub and stretched her legs. The ache in her thighs reminded her that she'd been carrying tension all day, longer than that. She fantasized about Graham. She imagined they were making love and lying in each other's arms. After, they would talk about everything—politics, music, whatever they read. She imagined them making love again and curled into him. She brought her vibrator into the tub and climaxed quickly. Fully relaxed, she submerged deeper until only her face hovered above the water, the city sounds dulled into nothing but muffled pulses in the distance.

A distinct sadness washed over her. She missed David. Still, she had a sickening feeling, a kind of nausea. Was it because she conjured up Graham? Was she betraying David? She'd had this anxious, nauseous pit in her stomach before. In this case, it was guilt and heartache.

In those moments, Hannah realized she had forgotten about David and wished to be with Graham. She has not missed David lately, yet she still experienced pangs of unbidden grief. Hannah had let someone else enter her consciousness. She had a massive crush on Graham and wanted him in every way. Hannah hated how clichéd that sounded, even in her head. But it was true. She was attaching herself to a new love interest for the first time.

Hannah didn't need to miss David anymore by being glued to him, to the exclusion of falling in love again and living her life. She thought, *I can honor his memory without foreclosing on living a life with someone else. I am not betraying or cheating on David. The memory of him stays intact.* Anyway, he would want her to be happy and not sacrifice her life in mourning for him. "I'm not getting any younger," she murmured under her breath. She opened her eyes and stared at the ceiling. The tiles above her had many slight cracks, just enough to remind her that even homes age.

She reached for her phone on the tub's edge—not to scroll but to reread the notes she had jotted down earlier. She had been organizing her thoughts for the full feature article on Dr. Jo—not just facts or quotes, but questions—personal ones, some new ones that she contemplated, and others that she had answered and reviewed in her mind.

Now, submerged to her collarbones, she imagined Dr. Jo sitting across from her, as she had done during their scheduled meetings. The doctor was calm, steady, and warm as can be. Elegant yet grounded, she had a mind like a scalpel.

What would she write to Dr. Jo from London? How would the article be received when it was published? Would Dr. Jo be happy and proud of the outcome? *Will she be as delighted when she reads the full article as when I read a condensed version to her?*

Hannah thought of David. He had loved baths, too. They used to crowd into tiny tubs in even tinier apartments, two knees knocking, limbs slipping beneath the surface.

She ran a wet hand over her face and inhaled the Dead Sea salts and the rose bath oils she had added to the water. Hannah knew that if she let herself, she could spiral out of control. Her mind had this tendency—call it writer's wiring—to dig tunnels in the dark and go down the rabbit hole. She learned that the fear of fear itself is the worst thing. But that night she tried something different.

She sat upright. The water sloshed gently around her ribs. *What would it mean to live without ghosts? Not to erase the past but to understand it. Not to avoid pain, but to speak to it—invite it in for tea, be well acquainted, then let it go when it is ready to leave.*

She wasn't sure she believed in catharsis, but she learned to breathe through the ache and be present, even when it hurt.

She stood, toweled off slowly, then wrapped herself in a thick robe and padded across the tile floor. The chill met her ankles, but she didn't mind.

Back in bed, her journal lay open. She wrote at the top of the page, "Trauma lives in the silence between stories." Then, underneath it, she wrote in smaller, hesitant script, "It's time to stop being afraid of my own."

She closed the book, shut the light, and turned toward sleep.

Chapter 15: Echoes From Ella

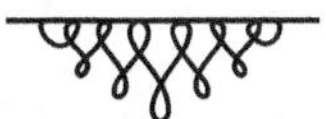

Hannah opened the closet door in her bedroom and reached for the top shelf. The shoebox, dusty and sagging in the middle, was still there, held together with a large, tired rubber band that had left an indentation across the faded cardboard lid. The name of the shoe store was still visible in block letters across the top: Florsheim—Broadway & 87th.

The box, labeled "Ella" in faded ink, had been a fixture in her closet for years—a silent sentinel of her past. Addie had given it to Hannah on her 21st birthday with a strange mixture of relief and ritual. "These belonged to your biological mother. She wanted you to have them when you were ready."

Hannah had touched the lid, then recoiled. "I'm not ready." *Not yet.* Hannah had resented Ella's absence before she understood or was aware of it. She had shoved the box into the closet, tucked behind out-of-season coats and boots she never wore, and pretended it wasn't there.

But now she was 35. She felt emboldened by everything Dr. Jo had helped her uncover, along with Zach and the Yellow Diary. Hannah felt an irresistible urge to confront the contents of the shoebox. She was finally ready.

She momentarily held the box to her chest before sitting cross-legged on the bed, her back against the headboard. She slipped off the rubber band, careful not to snap it. She lifted the lid with deliberate hesitation, uncertain what waited inside.

The smell hit her first. Mothballs. Her entire childhood, the attic of their house had smelled like naphthalene.

Inside the box were layers of airmail envelopes and onion-skin paper folded into tight rectangles, some still sealed. There were about 20 letters, each marked in pencil with a date and a number. A faint scent of drugstore perfume and the mildew of time clung to the pages.

On top of the letters was a brief note in Addie's handwriting: "I never read them. These were passed to me when we adopted you. I was told to give them to you on your 21st birthday. I hope you understand why I waited. Love, Mom."

Hannah sat still, holding that note. The word "Mom" disarmed her. Addie didn't usually call herself that so plainly. But here it was. Simple. Certain.

Ella's letters were raw and beautiful. Sometimes poetic, sometimes rambling, they weren't always coherent, but they were full of love, guilt, longing, and sadness. Ella hadn't abandoned Hannah, not really. She'd been young, alone, and scared. The letters traced a woman trying to grow up while mourning her mother, whom she lost, and a daughter she couldn't keep.

Around the fourth letter, Hannah began to sob; not the tight, clean tears of sadness, but the messy, gut-deep weeping of recognition. Her mother had thought of her every single day. She had wanted her to know the truth, not just the facts, but the feelings.

Amidst the letters lay a collection of relics: a delicate silver locket, another stack of yellowed letters, and a single photograph. Hannah picked up the photo, her fingers tracing the image of a young woman with dark, wavy hair and piercing green-gray eyes—eyes that mirrored her own. On the back, in plain script, was written "Ella, 1983."

She unfolded one of the letters, the paper brittle beneath her touch. The handwriting was fluid, each word carefully chosen:

My Dearest Hannah,

   I hope this letter finds you healthy and happy. There are truths I've longed to share, shadows from my past that have shaped the woman I've become and, inevitably, the woman you are becoming.

The letter continued, revealing fragments of Ella's life—her struggles, passions, and the circumstances that led to Hannah's adoption. Tears blurred her vision as Hannah absorbed each revelation, feeling an intimate connection to the mother she had never known.

One letter addressed to Hannah's adoptive mother stood out among the other letters. Curiosity piqued, she read:

Dear Addie Glass,

Entrusting Hannah to you was the most wrenching decision of my life. Yet, I find solace in knowing your love and guidance embrace her. Please tell her about me when the time is right. Let her know that my absence was not a choice made lightly.

Hannah ached with a complex blend of sorrow, longing, and gratitude. She realized that the narratives she'd constructed about her origins were incomplete and lacked the depth of her mother's perspective.

Hannah pulled out one letter at random. It was dated 1989 and written by Ella:

To the child, I could not raise—

Hannah stopped. Her breath caught like a stitch in her ribs. She felt like she was being yanked apart in a mental tug-of-war. Hannah wasn't sure she could keep reading. But she did.

Dear Hannah,

By now, you must have wondered who your father was. The truth is, I don't know his whereabouts. He doesn't even know my last name. What happened between us was neither brutal nor beautiful. I was young. We had gone out a few times, and I agreed to kiss him. Things got out of hand. I thought I said no, but I'm not sure what happened. He didn't force me, but I wasn't ready. And I don't think he even noticed. He was a good man—a college student from a good family. I don't think he meant any harm. I think we were just two young people who didn't know what we were doing—or what the consequences might be.

I don't know who he is, but if you ever want to find him, I will understand and not be sorry.

Love, Ella

Hannah stared at the paper. She reread it. Then again. Her hand reached automatically for her phone. She dialed.

Addie answered on the third ring. "Sweetheart?"

"Mom, did you ever know anything about my father?"

A pause. "No," Addie said gently. "Only that Ella didn't want to talk about him. And that she asked us not to ask either."

Hannah let the silence stretch. "OK," she said. "I just needed to hear that."

"I know, love."

"Thanks, Mom, I love you."

After she hung up, Hannah returned the letter to the box and pulled out the next one. She would read every single one—tonight, tomorrow, it didn't matter. These letters were her roots. They were her beginning.

Not just mystery, but memory. Not just absence, but a voice. She curled back on the bed, holding the box like something sacred.

That night Hannah dreamed that her birth mother wrote her the following letter:

We have been lost to one another for so long. I look at the moon and know that my name has been scattered in the wind to most people. But to you, I am not gone. Just as I prepared to turn away from the moon to sleep peacefully, my friend, Memory rises from the fine, powdery dust of so many new moons. Memory takes my arm and leads me through a labyrinth of flowers atop a hillock covered with dense trees, and we meander through deep and remote areas of the mind where collective Memory resides. And that is where I find myself among my ancestors.

My loved ones. Past, present, and future. That is where I found my mother's, grandmothers' and great-grandmothers' breath in every word. "I remember you," I tell them. "I love you. I have not forgotten." I take joy and comfort in remembering my ancestors. Then you appear, Hannah to say that the pain of traumas you have endured lessens with time and connection. By reconnecting, we are not lost to one another.

Memory reintroduced me to the stories of my life when so many cruelties were taking place. Ancestors whisper stories and secrets in the sounds and music of their names, in the sparkles of their laughter, in the etchings of their pictures left behind for families and history books.

Memory offers swatches of pain and grief that live on. Grief always, in some way, accompanies us since humans are imperfect and life is challenging. There are times when the presence of sorrow is acute: a partner or parent dies, a home turns to ash in a fire, a war rages, a marriage dissolves, and we find ourselves alone. And we are lost.

At some point in time, and beyond time, we all struggle to find a purpose in our lives, and at other times, we learn that the purpose isn't the struggle. The struggle was a defining moment of awareness, and resilience.

Sometimes, it hurts to hear our words and to look closely at them, even as Memory holds my hand. If you look hard enough, you will notice conscious thought and reflection in the emotional pain.

Ultimately, loss opens the way for meaning and a new encounter. I'm teaching you that we don't need to be lost to one another. Memory beckons me to whisper stories to tell you. Some good, some bad. Some joyful. Some tearful. They are all critical.

Thank you for being all the things that define each of us: strong, brave, wonderstruck, kind, gifted, broken, loyal, foolish, talented, and weak. Thank you for being you.

With Love,

Your Mother

Hannah awakened with a start. She was sweaty, clammy, and agitated. She felt a pit in her stomach—the heartbroken, crestfallen pang of longing. Her mind was a whirr. The dream felt like a gift and a trick. Hannah wondered what it meant. The voices in her mind were unrelenting: *I should not have read Ella's letters. I am working too hard on this article. Is Ella dead? In heaven? Or alive? Where is she? Did she love me? How does she define Love? Does birthing a child mean that you love them? Ella gave me away. Is there a paradox inherent to love and abandonment that I am missing? Nothing makes sense. I will find her someday. Not now.*

"Yikes! Got to get to the airport this morning," she muttered. The mental chatter was numbing.

Hannah arrived at JFK International Airport in ample time for her flight to London. She sat in an overstuffed armchair in the British Airways lounge, nursing a glass of wine and munching on a mix of mini pretzels and spicy corn nuts. During the two hours before boarding the flight, Hannah equivocated about whether the *Currents* article was finished or if it still needed work. She was growing tired of the project with which she had been entirely preoccupied for the last two months. Hannah knew she was perfectionistic and had a proclivity towards overthinking and overworking. *It's easier to goof off and procrastinate,* she thought, since Sophie, her editor, had not imposed a hard deadline. Hannah had worked assiduously, and Dr. Jo loved what she'd heard! So, Hannah reread the piece and felt genuinely satisfied with it.

She hoped to clear her mind and enjoy London, being fully present. *It's been two months,* she thought, *and it's a stellar article, so there's no reason to perseverate and rehash. Just forget about it while you're in London,* she told herself. She reviewed it once more on her laptop and decided it was time to send it to Sophie. Hannah informed her with a text message.

While Hannah was seated on the plane, before taking off, Sophie texted back: "Story received. Just what the doctor ordered! Fabulous."

Chapter 16: In the Flesh

Hannah stepped through the arrivals gate at Heathrow Airport, her heart thudding so hard she was sure the people jostling past could hear it. The static-lit air was thick with voices, rolling luggage, and long-awaited greetings.

Clutching the handle of her suitcase, she scanned the crowd of expectant faces. There—just beyond —stood Graham Pauly, precisely as she had seen him dozens of times on her screen, and yet still so startlingly real. He was tall and handsome, not a problem framed by pixels, and not buffered by screen lag. Graham's eyes met hers and lit up in recognition. A smile broke across his face—that warm, crooked grin she knew so well—and Hannah felt every nerve in her body come alive.

She took a tentative step forward, then another. Hannah was weaving through the cluster of travelers, separating them. Her vision blurred with tears of anticipation, but she kept her gaze locked on Graham. *He's here. I'm here. This is real.* The weeks of Zoom calls and late-night WhatsApp confessions all converged into this single, electric moment. Two months of messages, stolen hours, and exciting confessions led to this: real air, real skin, approaching a tangible presence.

"Hannah!" Graham called, his voice carrying over the hum. It was both strange and perfect to hear him say her name outside of a phone or laptop speaker. She laughed through a sob as she closed the final gap between them.

For a minute, neither of them moved. Then Hannah's pace accelerated until she reached him. She dropped her bag and wrapped her arms around him as if gravity had magnetically snapped them into place.

Graham caught her with both arms and pulled her tightly against his chest. She stepped into his embrace as he wrapped her up tightly against him, and Hannah melted into the solidity of his body. He smelled of woodsy and citrus notes, flooding her with a pleasant sensation. Her cheek pressed against the soft wool of his coat right over his heart, and she felt its rapid beating match her own. Graham's arms trembled momentarily as if he, too, was overwhelmed by the magnitude of the moment.

Neither spoke. It wasn't necessary. The feeling was mutual, massive, and honest.

"You're here," he said, brushing a strand of hair from her cheek. "And you are so much more beautiful in 3D than I imagined."

Hannah smiled helplessly, fully. "So are you." She felt heat rise to her cheeks. They were both a little bashful now, grinning like fools. It was the joyful awkwardness of two people who had already declared love from afar but were now physically close for the first time. She bit her lip, trying to find something witty to say to break the spell before she started crying in earnest. But words failed her. Instead, she let her hand slide to his neck and gently pulled him toward her. Graham understood.

He dipped his head, eyes never leaving hers until the last second, and their lips met in a soft, trembling kiss. It was a first kiss, but it felt like a homecoming. Hannah sighed against his mouth, relief, and elation coursing through her. Graham's lips were warm and familiar in an entirely new way. He tasted faintly of mint, and his kiss was gentle, almost reverent, then slowly growing firmer as their pent-up longing found an outlet. Hannah's heart soared. She curled her fingers into the lapel of his coat, holding him close, standing on tiptoe to deepen the kiss a little more. A tiny sound, a seductive coo, escaped her, and she felt Graham smile against her lips.

"We did it. We're together." His voice wavered on that last word, betraying how excited he was.

Then he kissed her again. Lightly at first, more a confirmation than a claim. And when her body leaned in, it was a yes that she hadn't even meant to say.

They kissed repeatedly. Hannah loved the solid press of his chest, the warmth of his mouth, the certainty of desire in his touch.

When they finally drew back just enough to see each other's faces, Graham kept his hands gently on her shoulders. His blue-gray eyes, more vivid in person, searched hers worriedly.

"Hello, Love," he said, voice low and unsteady. "You're here." He spoke the words like a marvel, as if he had to convince himself she wasn't a dream.

Hannah let out a sultry laugh. "I'm here," she managed. They both felt surreal. Hannah's eyes welled up as she noted faint tears glistening in Graham's eyes. She had seen every nuance of his expressions in their countless video calls, but seeing those eyes up close, welling with tears for her, was a new kind of exquisite. She lifted a hand to his face without thinking. "And you're real," she whispered, brushing her fingertips along his jaw where a hint of stubble caught the light.

Graham noticed and flushed, smiling while reaching down to grab her dropped suitcase. He still thought of himself as an awkward, gangly teenager. He had outgrown that stage a long time ago. Still, although he had a way with women and never had any problem attracting them, he had never thought of himself as a handsome hunk that women would lust after. His modesty made him much more appealing. Hannah was unusually gorgeous, which made him feel a little insecure.

"Come on," he said kindly. "Let's get out of this madhouse." Still, he kept his other arm securely around her waist as they started to walk, as if afraid she might disappear if he let go. Hannah leaned into him, tucking herself under his arm. It felt natural, as if they had walked side by side a hundred times before.

Hannah briefly noticed the distinctive airport smell of coffee, jet fuel, and the perfumes of thousands of travelers. Still, all she registered was the comforting pressure of Graham's arm and the occasional squeeze of his hand on her hip. Every few steps, they glanced at each other and exchanged incredulous smiles and glances that felt like confessions. It was as though they had to keep confirming, *It's you; we're arm-in-arm now.*

Now and then, Hannah's nerves flickered up again, a voice in her head whispering that it was all too much, too fast, and too good to last. She kept these thoughts to herself, hoping Graham did not perceive her sweaty palm and chewed fingernails as she clutched his hand. When she looked over and saw his jaw tighten and brow furrow, she realized she wasn't the only one wondering if they were getting ahead of themselves. The thought was comforting and reassuring: he was human too, and they were both afraid. Graham caught her watching him, and he smiled through pursed lips as he squeezed her hand, as if to say, *I know we'll figure it out.*

Outside, London greeted them with brisk autumn air. The sky was a fluff of low clouds that threatened imminent rain. Hannah shivered pleasantly as the cool breeze hit her, and Graham instantly pulled her closer. "Are you all right?" he asked, concern flickering over his face.

"I'm perfect," she assured him, and she meant it. Jet lag and nerves aside, she felt buoyant erotic energy coursing through her veins. She was standing on British soil, breathing London air for the first time in years, but more importantly, she was with Graham. The reality of that fact kept catching her off guard and making her want to giggle or cry simultaneously.

They walked to the car park where Graham had left his car. The city's sounds welcomed them—distant car horns, a peal of laughter ringing. Hannah was hyper-aware of every detail: the damp air hinting at rain, the rhythmic click of her suitcase wheels on the pavement. Everything felt significant, as if London knew this was a special day for them.

Graham led her to a compact navy-blue car. He opened the passenger door for her and stowed her suitcase in the back. As he slid into the driver's seat, he exhaled a long breath and looked at her across the console. "Hannah," he said, almost laughing as he ran a hand through his dark hair, "I still can't believe you're here beside me. I am dumbfounded."

She turned in her seat to face him, drawing one knee up. "I know. I keep thinking I'll wake up on a plane mid-flight, and this will be a dream." Tentatively, she reached out and laid her hand over his, where it rested on the gearshift. His fingers interlaced with hers smoothly as if they'd done it a million times. The gesture made Hannah's chest ache with happiness. Hannah was a physical, affectionate creature. She needed to be touched and embraced to thrive.

"If it were a dream," Graham said softly, "I wouldn't feel this real." He lifted their joined hands, their fingers intertwined, and he kissed the back of hers. Hannah felt the warmth of his lips and the gentle scratch of stubble, and she smiled, a blush warming her cheeks, while her body tingled with desire.

They remained there a moment, hands clasped. Hannah wanted to say so much about how he looked even more handsome in person, about how grateful she was for every midnight conversation that had led them here, about the wild hope she felt for what might come next, but her thoughts were a jumble. In the end, she just squeezed his hand. "Thank you for meeting me," she said. It carried all the unsaid things in it.

"Where else would I be?" He gave her that heart-stopping smile again. Then, with a playful glint, he added, "Besides, I've been told I'm responsible for looking after you on this trip. Direct orders from a certain Mr. Levi."

Hannah tittered. "Ah, yes, Grandpa's directives." The word Grandpa felt strange on her tongue. She had only recently learned to associate it with Zachary Levi, a man she had never met but whose actions were now changing her life. "I suppose I should let you play the dutiful host then," she teased gently.

Graham's expression softened. "I'm happy to, duty or otherwise." He started the car and pulled out of the space. As they drove from the airport and merged onto the highway, dusk began to fall, painting the sky in smoky purples and blues. London proper awaited in the distance.

For a few minutes, they rode in companionable silence. Hannah watched the scenery flash by—red double-decker buses lumbering along, a glimpse of the Thames as they crossed a bridge, rows of tidy brick houses, and flashes of green parkland. It was a blur of a new city, but Graham's presence made it all feel oddly familiar, as if she belonged here with him. She realized her hand was still in his, resting on the center console, and neither intended to let go.

Eventually, Graham spoke, his tone turning a bit more serious. "How are you feeling about tomorrow?" He did not need to elaborate; Hannah knew he was referring to her impending meeting with her grandfather, Zachary Levi.

Hannah felt uncomfortable; her earlier giddiness tempered into nerves again. "I'm not sure," she admitted. "Excited. And anxious." She stared at the blur of billboards and neon lights appearing as evening fell. "I mean, I've imagined meeting him many times since I found out. But imagining and doing it are two different things."

Graham gave her hand a reassuring squeeze. "He's a good man, Hannah. You know, I've known him for ten years. He has been like a father to me, especially since I lost my parents during COVID. I wouldn't have arranged all this if I didn't love and trust him."

She nodded. Graham had told her as much on a call: Zach had been a mentor and friend to him, and he cared deeply about doing right by Hannah.

"I know. It's not that I'm afraid of him. It's more that I am afraid of what I'll feel. This is a big piece of a very head-spinning puzzle."

He glanced at her; concern etched on his brow. "You don't have to do anything you're not ready for. If you want more time."

"No," Hannah cut in softly. "This is all happening at lightning speed. The whole thing: The diaries, the chest, Zach. You. I don't know how I'm supposed to feel. I'm worried that you think I came for a package deal; the American woman who shows up just in time to claim her inheritance."

Graham looked at her for a moment. "I know you're not a gold digger, but I'd be lying if I said the thought didn't cross my mind when Zach first mentioned you. Not because of you, but because it all came out of nowhere. Even though he had been looking for you, suddenly his granddaughter, the woman I can't stop thinking about, materializes."

"That's fair," Hannah said, cracking a smile. Although his admission that he thought she might have been a gold digger stung, as did his cooler tone of voice.

"I'm just trying to stay afloat. You dropped into my life like a storm system. I'm also trying to manage my experience," Graham added defensively.

"I understand a lot is going on for both of us. I want to meet him. Truly. After everything I've learned about my family in the past weeks, I need to see him. I need to hear the story of what happened from someone who was there." She paused, then whispered, "And he's, my grandfather. My blood. I've lived my whole life not knowing that. I can't ignore it now."

Graham nodded. "All right. Just remember, you don't have to face it alone. I'll be right there with you if you want."

A wave of gratitude swelled in Hannah. She released his hand and looped her arm through his as he drove, leaning her head on his shoulder momentarily. He briefly tilted his head to rest against hers, carefully keeping his eyes on the road. "Thank you," she said. "For everything, Graham. For helping me find the truth. For being here."

She felt him press a kiss to the top of her head. "There's nowhere else I'd rather be."

Once at Graham's Islington flat, exhaustion came over Hannah. After a simple dinner, which neither of them tasted much, they were too busy stealing awed glances at one another. Hannah was so bone-tired from travel and emotions, but happier than she could ever remember. Graham guided her to the guest bedroom, ever the gentleman. Despite his intense attraction and reluctance to part from her, he left the room so she could get ready for bed. When he returned a few minutes later to see if she needed anything, she was fast asleep, fully clothed, with the scent of him still on her clothes. He lay down beside her, spooning, and fell asleep.

The next morning, they would have loved to luxuriate in each other's arms, explore each other's bodies, and spend the day in bed. Instead, they hurriedly dressed in their respective rooms, grabbed a coffee, and headed out the door.

Chapter 17: Lineage and Linkage

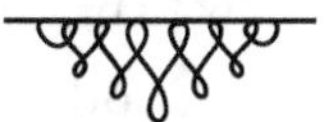

Hannah stood in front of a quaint townhouse in Hampstead, her stomach doing nervous flips. Autumn flowers spilled from window boxes, and the brick facade was adorned by creeping ivy. In just moments, she would come face to face with the man who had loved her grandmother and, improbably, turned out to be her grandfather. Hannah's palms were damp despite the wind chill.

Graham was by her side. As they climbed the steps to the front door, he gently touched the small of her back. "You ready?" he asked under his breath.

Hannah swallowed hard. "As I'll ever be." She smiled meekly and reached out to ring the doorbell before her courage failed.

Footsteps sounded from within, and then the door opened. An older man stood there, leaning lightly on a cane. He was slender and tall, with snowy white hair neatly combed back. His eyes struck Hannah immediately, a clear hazel, remarkably bright, yet soft. There was a moment of mutual searching: his gaze found her face, and Hannah saw a whole flurry of emotions cross his features—hope, trepidation, and overwhelming tenderness all at once. Hannah fleetingly thought their anxious emotions mirrored one another, cut from the same cloth.

"Hello," the man said in a gentle, yet firm voice. "You must be Hannah."

"Yes," she managed. "I'm Hannah." Her voice wavered. "Are you Zachary?"

The older man's lips curved into a humble smile. "Please, call me Zach." Then he seemed to reconsider and added softly, "Or whatever you feel comfortable with." There was a catch in his voice. Hannah realized he was still holding himself, unsure if he should hug her.

In that instant, Hannah's nervousness dissolved. Here was someone who was also vulnerable and not sure how to bridge the years of unknown between them. She took a step forward. "It's good to meet you, Zach," she said. Her voice came out steadier than she felt. On impulse, she opened her arms a little. "Can I—may I hug you"?

Zach's smile trembled, and his hazel eyes shone. "I would like that very much," he said.

Hannah moved into him and gently wrapped her arms around his frail frame. He felt solid but fragile at once, so she was careful not to jostle him. Zach released his cane to return the embrace, folding her against him. She felt his hand stroke her hair in a grandfatherly gesture that constricted her heart. He relaxed into the hug, with a bit of resistance in letting go, the way people who are alone and not touched enough do. The hug felt oddly familiar despite having just met, as if some part of her recognized him. *This is family,* she thought. *Blood calling to blood.*

"Welcome, Hannah," he murmured near her temple. His voice was thick with emotion. "I have waited a long time for this day."

Hannah tightened her hug briefly, eyes shut. "Me too," she admitted in a whisper. In truth, she hadn't known what she was waiting for most of her life, a missing piece she could never name. Now, standing here, she felt that piece click into place.

"Graham, my boy," Zach greeted him, patting his hand. "Thank you for bringing her."

Graham nodded, warmly placing his hand on Zach's shoulder. Hannah felt another wave of gratitude that Graham had been the bridge between her and this newfound family.

"Come inside, both of you," Zach urged, realizing he still had them on the stoop. "No sense catching a cold out here."

They entered the house. The interior was cozy, filled with warm lamplight, and the subtle aroma of old books and freshly brewed coffee. Hannah's eyes took in the surroundings, shelves crammed with leather-bound volumes, a mantel with framed photographs (she wondered if any were of Maria or her mother as a baby), a vase of white lilies on an end table. The living room was elegant and masculine in style: comfortable, worn armchairs, a tartan blanket draped over a sofa, and lace curtains filtering the daylight. It struck Hannah that this was the home of someone intellectual and sentimental; Zach had so many memories carefully arranged in this space.

"Have a seat, please," Zach said, gesturing to the sofa. "Make yourselves comfortable. Can I get you tea or coffee? I've just made a pot." He moved with a slight shuffle, leaning on his cane, but determined to play the host.

Hannah was about to insist she was fine, but Graham spoke up, ever tactful. "I'd love some tea, thank you." He caught Hannah's eye, silently encouraging her to accept the hospitality—it might put Zach more at ease.

"Yes, tea sounds nice," Hannah added with a forced smile. The truth was her nerves were still fluttering; wrapping her hands around a warm cup might steady them.

"Good, good," Zach nodded. "Please, sit."

As he headed toward the kitchen nook, Graham helped Hannah remove her coat, and they sat together on the sofa. Hannah's fingers twisted together in her lap. She glanced at a cluster of photos on the side table. One showed a much younger Zachary—in his 30s—standing beside another man in academic robes (Oxford or Cambridge, she guessed). Another was an old, sepia-toned picture of a stern-looking woman in 1930s fashion—Zach's mother or another relative. Hannah's gaze halted on a small silver frame at the center: it held a faded photograph of a beautiful, dark-haired young woman laughing candidly as she leaned against a lamppost. She recognized Maria, her young grandmother, who looked barely out of her teens, her smile carefree and radiant, free of the ghosts that shadowed her. Hannah gingerly picked up the frame, almost afraid to touch such a precious fragment of the past.

Zach returned, carrying a tray with a teapot and cups, just as Hannah had examined the photo. He was surprisingly agile for his age, and Hannah now understood how he could still live alone without assistance. Zach paused, following her gaze. "That was your grandmother, Maria, in 1950," he said softly. There was a fond, faraway tone to his voice. "I took that picture of her. She didn't know I was snapping it—she was laughing at some joke I'd made. It was one of the rare times I caught her off guard, genuinely happy in the moment." Zach smiled wistfully as he set the tray down on the coffee table. "She was alive. Vibrant. Despite everything that had happened, Maria had this spirit about her. A bright light. It drew people in. I know it drew me in." He sank into the armchair across from the sofa, leaning his cane against the side. His recollection hung in the air momentarily, and none of them spoke.

Zach cleared his throat gently. "I hardly know where to begin, Hannah. There's so much I want to tell you." He gave a soft, apologetic laugh. "And I imagine you have many questions."

She nodded, meeting his eyes. "I do. But start with whatever you think I should know about you, about Maria." She paused. "About why none of us knew about you until now." There was no accusation in her tone, only a plaintive curiosity.

Zach's face grew somber. He took a long breath. "Fair enough." He cradled his cup of coffee, staring momentarily into it gathering his thoughts. "I'd like to tell you about the woman I knew, your grandmother, and our time together after the war. And I will explain why she never spoke of those days." He looked up, eyes earnest. "Some of it may be painful to hear, but I think you're ready, yes?"

He handed her a cup of tea, then one to Graham, then settled carefully into his armchair. For a moment, they drank in silence. The tea was hot and intense.

Zach glanced at Hannah's face, really looked at her, and a flicker of something shifted in his expression, a trace of a wistful smile. "You look like her; it is uncanny, and you are as pretty as she was," he said.

Hannah held his gaze. "Maria?"

He nodded. "There's something in your eyes. She used to sit like that, too. Quiet, waiting. Listening before speaking."

"I thought it would be more respectful to let you speak first."

Zach chortled with exaggerated, feigned surprise. "OK, fair enough!"

Hannah felt Graham beside her, steady and silent. Zach turned to her. "Maria was 18. I was a 21-year-old law student. She worked in a library in London just after the war. She was quiet but brilliant. She could catalogue books like they were people, remembering their stories, grouping them by character, not subject. I remember thinking it was strange at first. But it made sense to her and it was a mental game she enjoyed."

He paused. "She had been through more than most people could survive. She rarely spoke about it. But you could see it in her eyes—a watchfulness, as if always measuring whether a place was safe."

"I started visiting her whenever I could during mutual breaks," Zach continued. "At first, it was easy talk; banter about books, the weather, silly observations about the people reading in the library. But little by little, she opened. I learned she was living in a sort of hostel for young refugees. She had a sharp mind and an incredible appetite for learning, but the war cut off her formal education. She had read everything she could get her hands on in that library."

Hannah listened, rapt. Maria had been a studious, intense young woman rebuilding herself.

Zach's eyes crinkled. "I was not surprised. Books were her solace and her teachers." He sighed, and his tone deepened. "Over the months, our friendship grew into something more. We fell in love, slowly, then all at once.

By 1950, Maria and I were inseparable." He glanced at Graham and gave a self-deprecating smile. "I won't embarrass our young friend here with too many romantic details but suffice it to say, we were very much in love—heart, mind, and body."

Graham chuckled, holding up a hand. "Don't mind me." He was also riveted and invested in the story, squeezing Hannah's hand gently as they listened.

Zach's smile faded as he continued wistfully. "Those were some of the happiest years of my life. But they were hard, too. Maria carried a lot of pain inside. She suffered with nightmares and flashbacks, although we did not have the words for sensory flashbacks back then. There were nights she woke up screaming, and all I could do was hold her until she calmed. She rarely spoke directly about what she had been through. I knew only fragments: that she had been in hiding as a child, that she had seen terrible things. She always said, 'The past is buried. I want to keep it that way.'"

Hannah felt a familiar pang; those words resonated with the hush her living Gran always put on anything related to the war or her childhood. "Yesterday will sleep so that I may wake," Maria had written in her diary. The theme of burying the past ran deep in both Hannah's mother's family and her adoptive family. Hardly a coincidence, since both grandmothers were Holocaust survivors and had what we now know as post-traumatic stress disorder (PTSD).

"She was stronger than anyone I knew," Zach said proudly. "To have endured all she did and still be able to love. It was remarkable. But that strength had a flip side. Part of it came from sealing away the hurt, locking it behind an iron door. And she was determined never to open that door again." He paused. "Even if that meant shutting out people who loved her."

Zach's gaze dropped. Hannah could see the emotion on his face, decades-old heartbreak, still tender. She noticed she clenched her fists and jaw, too. She breathed, consciously relaxing and resetting her anxiety meter. "What happened?" she asked gently.

Zach took another sip of coffee to steady himself. "In 1950, when we were happiest, Maria moved to Berlin. She couldn't get comfortable in England, and ironically, it was easier for Jews to live in post-war Germany than to live in England. In Germany, people were afraid to be antisemitic. They compensated by being overly kind and helpful to Jewish survivors. The collective German guilt was fierce for a while. Until there was enough time to forget what happened and reinvent history."

"Frankly, I think she was scared by our love relationship. She was damaged. I was hopelessly in love with her, and I was devastated that she left me. But as luck would have it, I had complicated legal cases in Berlin relating to monetary compensation—*Wiedergutmachung*, meaning 'to make good again,' for Holocaust survivors, and reclaiming of Jewish property for families that had survived the war and the wreckage. I was there frequently for extended periods. So, Maria and I had a stormy and intense relationship that continued until 1958. Those were the best years of my life..." His voice trailed off.

"I begged her to marry me, and I even bought her a ring. But she said no, that she was too damaged to be anyone's wife."

"*No?*" Hannah echoed, eyebrows rising in sympathy. She could only imagine how that felt for Zach.

Zach sighed heavily, his hands gripping his cup. "She told me she loved me and that I would make a wonderful father, but she refused to marry me. I was shocked and hurt. I couldn't understand it at the time. We quarreled. Eventually, she broke down and told me her reasons. She said she couldn't bear the idea of bringing a child into the world with so much darkness in her—the nightmares, the secrets, the blood in her past. She was convinced it would taint the baby or that she'd be an unfit mother because of her trauma. She felt I deserved a normal wife, life, family, and children."

Zach closed his eyes briefly, pained by the memory. "I tried to convince her otherwise. I begged her to let me help, to face the past together so we could be free of it. But that frightened her even more. Opening those old wounds, she just wouldn't."

"Of course, I didn't know she was pregnant in 1958. She broke up with me abruptly when she found out. I had a gut feeling she was pregnant because of the way she shut me out immediately without discussion. She admitted her pregnancy when I pressured her, but she left me anyway. I lost track of her and discovered years later, through mutual acquaintances, that she had moved to New York with her daughter, Ella, our daughter. I tried to reach her, but she didn't respond. It was not long before I understood that she wanted to release me from her love for me."

Hannah felt tears on her cheeks. She pictured Maria as beautiful and capable, pregnant and terrified that her trauma would somehow poison her child's life. This broke Hannah's heart.

"So, what did she do?" she whispered.

"Before she went to Berlin, she had already considered going to America. I wanted to go with her, but she forbade it. She preferred that I remember her as I knew her, not watch her fall apart. And that perhaps one day, if she healed, she would find me again, should I still be single, although that was unlikely, she thought." His voice cracked. "I didn't want to let her go, but she was resolute. Maria could be very insistent when she'd made up her mind."

A rueful smile touched Hannah's lips through her tears. "Yes. Stubborn and incorrigible. I must have inherited that trait from her." A moment of comic relief was a welcome respite from the achingly tragic disclosure.

Zach grinned, his eyes glistened. "It seems some traits do carry on." He drew a deep breath and continued.

"So, it turns out Maria and Ella emigrated to New York in 1965 with the sponsorship of two Jewish American organizations: the American Jewish Joint Distribution Committee, and the Hebrew Immigrant Aid Society–HIAS. She got on a ship bound for New York. Serendipitously, we had a mutual acquaintance, a source familiar to both of us, who told me he had never seen a sadder expression than hers as she waved from the deck. Everything else I know about her life there was secondhand, from people somehow connected to others who lived in Washington Heights, then a German-Jewish enclave in Manhattan. As a tailor and her own boss, Maria could manipulate her hours and do much of her work while Ella slept at night. She also attended school for Library Sciences a few hours a day while Ella was in school and eventually landed a decent job as a librarian in a Jewish day school in Riverdale, not far from where they lived. Sadly, Maria died of a ruptured appendix left unattended for too long. She was only 48 years old. Both mother and daughter were orphaned teenagers."

Chapter 18: Good and Wicked

Graham quietly set down his tea, the clink of porcelain sounding loud in the hush. Hannah reached for a tissue from a box on the table and dabbed at her eyes. "Maria raised my mother mostly in the States," Hannah said. "But she never told her about you, or anything. Mom only knew that Ella's father was 'gone' and that her mother had survived the war. But the details were always scant. Ella learned early not to ask because it upset her mother. I only know these details from reading the letters left to me that I just read a few weeks ago. Phew—this is a lot of information to absorb."

Zach nodded sadly. "I corresponded with Maria, you know, for a few years. She allowed that much. She sent me a letter when your mother was born to say she was healthy. I received another letter when she completed her degree in library science. We both love books, and that's where we met, in the library."

A silence fell, full of decades of longing and regret. Hannah found herself getting up and crossing to Zach's chair. On instinct, she knelt beside him and took his hand. "Zach," she said, trembling, "I'm so sorry. I'm sorry you and Maria went through all of this and that you missed so much. It seems unbearably cruel, all that wasted time."

Zach set his cup aside and placed his other hand over hers, enclosing her smaller hand in his warm, thin ones. "Meeting you now, knowing Maria's family, mends something in me," he said gently. "I won't pretend I haven't grieved what I lost. But seeing you here, grown into this compassionate, curious woman, comforts me. It's because a part of her life is in you."

Hannah felt tears spill over again, mixed with sorrow and gratitude. She squeezed his hand. "I feel like I'm just getting to know who she truly was and who I truly am, by extension."

"On that note," Zach continued, "Let me tell you more about Maria's parents. Her father, Wolf, was a Jewish man from Poland who studied engineering in France in his late teens. That man married Celeste, a French Roman Catholic, and they had Maria, who was born in 1929." Hannah felt a chill down her spine.

"Because she came from a family of influence, Celeste naïvely thought that her husband would be spared. She loved her husband and tried to protect him, but he was executed at Dachau, where he had been imprisoned and tortured by an SS officer. Months later, another SS officer hunted down Celeste, shot her in the head, and killed her. So, helping her Jewish husband was a crime punishable by death; so much for being a Jew lover."

Zach's eyes filled with sympathy at her evident distress. "Yes. Maria discovered the truth about her mother's activities as a child. She was with her mother in that Provençal village during part of the war. The diaries and letters you have can fill in details but let me summarize what Maria told me years later when we had a single night of honesty between us." He took a measured breath, clearly affected by the tale he was about to recount.

"In 1943, Celeste, Maria's mother, fled occupied Poland with young Maria, and made the dangerous journey to France, seeking refuge with her mother. Celeste hoped blood would outweigh ideology and that her mother would shelter her half-Jewish grandchild. It was horrible enough that the Nazis had murdered Celeste's husband for being a Jew. But she was wrong." His jaw tightened. "Dauphine—your great-great grandmother—refused to help her daughter, Celeste, and granddaughter, Maria. Horrified to have Jewish kin, she turned them away, even as the Nazis and collaborators were hunting down Jews in the area. Celeste had to hide Maria in the woods near the estate while she begged her mother for mercy."

Hannah was trembling, tears pouring down her face. She felt physically ill, grief-stricken, and dirty, as if contaminated by evil. She felt Graham's arm tighten protectively around her, and was grateful; she needed that anchor to the here and now as this grim history washed over her.

"Oh my God," she whispered shakily. "Oh my God, my great-great-grandmother was the epitome of evil. How does one even...ugh!" She trailed off, with disgust and angst, unable to wrap her mind around the story.

"Celeste fled with Maria," Zach continued. "They were in grave danger; the Nazis knew of the child's Jewish heritage and Celeste's attempt to save her Jewish husband. They were near Berlin when they captured and murdered Celeste. But Maria managed to escape, and was on the run till the end. She suffered at the hands of the Russian soldiers in March 1945, which she describes in gruesome detail in her diary." Hannah remembered.

"As I said, Celeste did not survive the war; she was caught and shot down on the spot.

Maria, at only 16, was alone and lost, unsure whether to go to Palestine, London, or America. London was the easiest fare. After the war, she received some money from the German government, which led her to end up here."

Hannah closed her eyes, absorbing the wave of sorrow for her great-grandmother Celeste, a woman she'd never known but to whom she owed her life. Celeste had sacrificed herself to save Maria. And Maria, as a girl, had witnessed unimaginable cruelty from her lineage.

No wonder Maria had nightmares. No wonder she never spoke to Zach about the past—how could she explain to a child or grandchild that racism, hatred, and evil ran in their family line alongside heroism and suffering?

Zach spoke softly now, in reverence. "Maria carried all of that inside her—the shame of her grandmother Dauphine, who sent her own kin to their death. Maria only told me the barest of details—but enough that I understood she believed there was a curse on her bloodline. She thought that the madness, the cruelty, might be inside her too, inherited like a disease. I tried to tell her she was nothing like Dauphine." He sighed. "But deep down, I think Maria feared that the darkness was part of her, and she was determined never to let it touch her child. That's one reason she never spoke of it and chose to leave me behind. She wanted to bury the family history."

Hannah felt a rush of empathy and heartbreak. Her grandmother had spent her life running from the specter of that legacy, trying to protect her daughter from it through silence and sheer will. And yet, the intense emotions had seeped through, like an invisible infusion—into nightmares, into unspoken anxieties that Hannah's mother inherited in the form of the need to give her baby up for adoption. Ella had the same feeling that Maria, her mother, had: that she wouldn't be capable of enough goodness to take care of her infant. That overprotectiveness and superstition were infused into Hannah's subconscious terror of a crying baby trapped in darkness. Were they cries of abandonment, or entrapment, or both? Were they her cries, her mother's, and her grandmother's? Were they metaphorical or actual? Both?

Emotional inheritance. Dr. Jo's phrase came to her mind. This was it, laid bare: the inheritance of both trauma and strength across generations.

Hannah drew a shaky breath and wiped her face. "All this time, I thought my family history was simply one of victims and survivors," she said quietly. "I never imagined I had an ancestor who was—" she hesitated, searching for the word, "—an oppressor."

Zach gave her a solemn look. "It's a heavy realization, I know. Maria bore that knowledge so your mother and you wouldn't have to. She wanted to shield you from the ugliness. But knowing it now can set you free in a way it never could for her."

Hannah frowned inquisitively. "How do you mean?"

Zach leaned forward, reaching out to clasp Hannah's hand once more. "My dear, you are the product of so many people's choices, the good and the bad. Maria's courage and her grandmother's cruelty are currents that run through your heritage. You've inherited Maria's resilience, Celeste's love, and yes, even

Dauphine and the Countess's formidable will—though you can use it for compassion rather than hate."

Zach's hazel eyes bore into hers with gentle intensity. "When we confront the truth of our past, even the parts that shame or horrify us, we take away its power to haunt us. Maria couldn't face it openly, and it haunted her. But you can. You can acknowledge it, speak it, and, in doing so, ensure that such darkness is not repeated. That it ends with you."

Hannah had not yet read the Countess's Red Diary and did not know they were blood relatives. She had brought it with her, planning to read it on the plane to London, but couldn't deal with the heaviness, watching in-flight movies instead. Now Hannah was trembling and biting her nails. Aware that she was holding her breath, the usual way she carried stress, Hannah, with concerted effort, quickly did a grounding exercise, focusing on being and feeling present. The notion was overwhelming yet oddly empowering: by knowing the whole story, she could be the one to break the cycle of silence and fear. Graham's hand found hers, holding tight, grounding her.

After a long pause, Hannah looked between Zach and Graham, seeing the concern and love on both their faces. She attempted to crack a smile. "I...I'm processing all of this. It's a lot," she confessed. "But, uh, I am glad I know...even the worst of it. Knowing where I come from, I feel more real and connected to my powerful ancestors: the good and the bad. And I haven't read the Countess's journal. Are we related to her also?"

"You'll see when you read the lengthy account that she was formidable. She was brilliant, iconoclastic, and way ahead of her time." Zach added. "From what we can tell, she was Dauphine's great-great-grandmother."

Zach nodded, a look of relief crossing his face. "You are your grandmother's granddaughter. She always sought the truth, even if she hid it from others. You have that same fire to understand." He then chuckled softly. "And from what I hear, you also have her talent for love. Maria would be happy to know you've found someone like young Graham here."

Hannah flushed and glanced at Graham, who turned slightly pink but smiled. It felt strange yet comforting to have her grandfather—this new grandfather—acknowledge her relationship. She realized with a start that Zach had been something of a matchmaker, introducing Graham to her in his letter. It was apparent that Zach loved Graham, who was like a son to him.

Graham cleared his throat, grinning. "I have a confession," he said lightly to Hannah, attempting to brighten the mood. "Zach told me before we got to know each other: 'She's a special one. You'll like her, I'm sure of it.' I suspect he undersold it quite a bit."

Hannah laughed, a welcome release of tension. She looked at Zach. "Oh, did you know? Trying to set me up before we'd even met?"

Zach raised his arms innocently. "I only wanted you to have a reliable guide in London. The rest, well, seeing you two now, I'd say the rest was meant to be." In truth, Zach had been very moved by Hannah's thoughtful and empathetic response to his letter.

There was a twinkle in his eye. The gentle tease and blessing in his words made Hannah's heart warm.

She rose and returned to Zach, leaning down to hug him tightly. "Thank you," she whispered. "For telling me everything. For trusting me with these truths. I know it must not be easy to revisit."

Zach returned the hug with surprising strength for his age and frail appearance.

"Thank you, Hannah, for listening. And for coming all this way to meet an old man. It has given me peace." She felt him press a kiss to her forehead, full of a grandfatherly love she'd never realized she missed until that moment.

Hannah embraced him and broke down weeping for all the years that she lost, not having a grandfather, and not having this incredible man for her grandfather. It felt at once extraordinary and tragic.

When they parted, Hannah noticed that it was twilight. She was so jet-lagged she didn't realize they had been talking for hours; it had felt like mere minutes. A soft rain had begun to patter against the windowpanes, typical London weather greeting the evening. Graham stood and stretched, then gathered the empty tea things on the tray to help tidy up.

"Leave it, my boy," Zach gently scolded him. "I'll take care of that later." Graham relented with a nod and set the tray back down.

Hannah held Zach's hand, reluctant to leave but knowing they all needed rest. "We should probably get going," she said softly. "But I'll be in London for a while. I'd love to come visit again, if you'd like that."

Zach's face brightened. "I would like that very much. You are welcome here anytime. There are many more stories to share, and I'd love to hear about your life, too. We haven't even touched on that." He gave her a proud once-over. "Maria's granddaughter, a writer, and a seeker. She would be so proud of you, Hannah. As am I. We are a family of storytellers. That is a good thing."

Hannah once again felt choked up, but with happiness this time. "That means the world to me," she said softly. She knew she wanted to tell him about her life, to fill him in on the granddaughter he never knew—her career, childhood memories, everything. And they would have time for that now, she hoped.

Graham helped Zach to his feet. At the door, Zach insisted on hugging Hannah again and firmly shook Graham's hand. "Take good care of her," Zach said to him, half serious, half joking.

"Always," Graham replied, throwing a warm glance at Hannah, making her heart flutter.

Chapter 19: The Lovers

The rain had eased to a slow drizzle as Hannah and Graham stepped outside into the blue dusk. They said their goodbyes, and Zach watched from the doorway until they were halfway down the block, waving gently. Hannah waved back one last time, her chest swelling with affection for the grandfather fate had finally brought into her life.

Hannah felt relieved that it went as well as she could have imagined. They walked arm in arm toward the car. The cool, damp air felt cleansing on her face. Her mind swirled with all she had learned: Maria's bravery and pain, Dauphine's dark legacy, and the hidden parts of her family story now revealed. It was a lot to accept. But she didn't manage it alone.

Graham pulled her close under the umbrella he'd popped open. "You all right?" he asked softly, peering at her with concern.

Instead of answering immediately, Hannah stepped in front of him, causing them both to halt on the quiet street. She slid her arms around his middle and rested her head on his chest. The umbrella tilted, the rain was misting the back of her hair, but she didn't care. Graham immediately enveloped her, one hand cradling the back of her head.

They stood silently under a streetlamp, enjoying this heavenly intimacy. Inwardly, she began to worry about what she would do if things didn't work out with Graham. Her mind was spinning with what-ifs. Hannah closed her eyes and listened to Graham's steady heartbeat. It was slower now than at the airport, with a strong and calming rhythm that anchored her in the present. His reassuring presence felt soothing and, in some way, magical.

Finally, she spoke, her voice muffled against his coat. "I have so many feelings right now; I don't even know where to start."

Graham rubbed her back soothingly. "Try me," he whispered.

She tilted her head up to look at him. His face was all gentle shadows and warm concern in the dim light. "I am sad, angry, hopeful, overwhelmed, and oddly peaceful." She gave a little laugh at the contradiction. Does that make sense?

A slow smile spread on Graham's face. "It does. It does." He bent to press a kiss to her forehead. "You, Hannah Glass, are a wonderful woman. Now I see even more where you get it from."

She smiled a genuine smile that reached her eyes. "I come from survivors and storytellers, and a Countess too." She shook her head in wonder. "It's a strange mix to manage, but it's mine."

Graham ran his hand along the softness of her cheek. "And you're not alone with it. I hope you know that Zach is here for you now." He hesitated just a beat, emotion lining his features. " So am I. If you'll have me."

Hannah felt a surge of warmth and love so strong it chased away the lingering darkness of the history they'd uncovered. She reached up and pulled his face down to hers, kissing him tenderly in what became heavy rain. The kiss was an affirmation of the present, of them, of life moving forward. When they parted, she rested her forehead against his, eyes shining. "I'm so grateful for you, Graham," she whispered. "I don't know how I would have faced all this without you holding my hand."

He thumbed away a tear from her cheek and gave a slight smile, lip curled up and away in the corner. It made him look very sweet, and also less perfect. "You would have managed, because you're amazing, but I'm glad you didn't have to go at it alone."

They stayed like that a moment longer, foreheads touching, exchanging soft breaths, and drawing strength from one another. Despite the heavy revelations of the day, Hannah felt light on her feet, buoyed by love and a newfound sense of happiness, even wholeness.

At last, Graham cleared his throat, a playful spark returning to his eyes. "What do you say we go home? Someone promised to show you the best fish and chips in London tonight. And after the day you've had, you deserve nothing less."

Hannah cracked up, recalling that he had made such a promise in one of their chats. Please leave it to Graham to remember and to know precisely when Hannah needed normalcy (and comfort food). "That sounds perfect," she agreed while giggling mischievously. Truthfully, they were not interested in eating food.

Hand in hand, they headed toward the car. Hannah glanced over her shoulder at the townhouse disappearing in the downpour. She felt a swell of emotion—gratitude, affection, a touch of sorrow—and then a calm acceptance. *Goodnight, Grandpa,* she thought warmly, knowing she would see him again soon.

As they drove, Hannah realized that this trip's vulnerability, anticipation, and bittersweet joy were weaving into her personal narrative. In the reflection of the window, she saw her face. For the first time, she recognized the woman she saw there: a woman shaped by romance and heartbreak, identity and inheritance, the love of those before her and the love she had finally allowed herself to embrace. Graham's hand found hers, fingers entwining in a familiar, reassuring knot.

Back at Graham's home, in his bedroom, Hannah lay on her side, her body half-draped across Graham's, her fingers tracing absent-minded patterns over his chest. The room smelled like a mix of sweat and rain. The window was open, the cool air mingling with the warmth of their skin. She was not thinking, at least not in the usual way. For once, her mind was not running ahead, bracing for an imminent threat and inevitable retreat. Hannah realized she was relaxed. It was an unfamiliar stillness, a quiet within herself she had not known before.

Graham shifted beneath her, his hand skimming along her arm, an effortless touch that might have been accidental if not for the way he lingered. "You OK? What are you thinking?" he whispered.

Something inside her, something she hadn't even known existed, was opening, yielding. They moved with quiet urgency, learning each other's rhythm with tenderness. It was not the pleasure that startled her but what came with it. A fullness. A surrender. And when she climaxed, she let herself fall into it, she gasped, not in shock or embarrassment but in the quiet, staggering realization that she had never, not once, felt like this with anyone before.

She wasn't sure how long she lay there afterward, her skin still humming, her body pliant against his. Graham had propped himself up on one elbow, watching her, brushing his fingers through the damp strands of her hair, kissing her face and neck.

"You look pensive," he murmured.

Hannah opened her mouth, then hesitated. How could she explain it? How could she verbalize and describe a feeling she had never experienced before? Everything she thought of saying sounded corny or sappy in her head.

Graham smiled. "You don't have to say it."

But she wanted to. She turned onto her side, lightly resting on Graham's chest, feeling his breath's slow, steady rhythm. "I didn't know sex, hmm, making love, could be like this," she meekly admitted. "This is a new experience for me." Her voice was quiet, but there was no shame, only surprise.

He traced his fingers along her jaw, studying her. "Like what?" A part of him was fishing for reassurance that he was a good lover and that she wanted him.

Hannah exhaled. "Like knowing and seeing each other. Like loving and being loved. Like being wildly attracted to you, the chemistry is physical and emotional. I feel so comfortable and relaxed. Being near you, breathing you in calms me. You are just fabulous for me." Hannah held onto the thought, knowing, for the first time, that she didn't need to run from it.

Hannah had always thought of sex as something to be done, pleasurable, but not something to be felt. It had been sweet but clumsy with David—two young bodies discovering each other with tenderness but without knowing what they were doing or why it mattered. They loved each other, but their lovemaking had been the groping, puerile, and ungratifying kind that belonged to first loves. It lacked the weight of mature intimacy.

After David, her relationships had been different. Darker. Her radar had been faulty, steering her toward the kind of men you'd try to forget the next morning: users, manipulators, charmers with nothing real to offer. The ones who didn't ask questions or bother to learn your name. Alpha males. Grifters. Narcissists. The kind who grabbed what they wanted and called you names if you hesitated. Men who took but never gave, who kept their wounds carefully hidden while exploiting hers.

Deep down, Hannah had known these men were toxic and not viable partners. She had let herself fall for them anyway, convincing herself that physical gratification was enough, that detachment was a form of control, and that if she kept the stakes low, she could never lose.

This was different. Graham was a grown-up. Graham was not someone she could outmaneuver, compartmentalize, or hold at arm's length. He saw her. He knew her anxieties. He was smart, and in sync. That feeling of being known was influencing her, both doing something and undoing something within. It was recognition. Mutuality and connection on every level. He was so tuned into her as if he'd known her all her life. She was two months into a virtual relationship, having just met Graham; yet she trusted him.

Unquestionably, Hannah knew Graham was a good guy. She felt it in the way he touched her, not just with want, but with certainty. He kissed her with hunger and longing, and as if he were listening and answering questions she had not yet spoken aloud. When she let herself go, and her body responded, it was not just physical. It was recognition.

She knew that Graham Pauly was the man she wanted to spend her life with. It was that simple.

Chapter 20: Countess Madeleine

In the first week that Hannah had been in London, she hadn't had a chance to read the Countess's diary. Between meeting family and her brilliant romance, there was just no inclination. Today, Graham had some work meetings to attend to and visit Zach.

Until Zach's disclosure, Hannah did not know if the diary belonged to a blood relative or had traveled alongside Maria's and other ancestral artifacts, folded into the same trunk and quiet legacy.

Hannah curled into the corner of the armchair by the window, the photocopied spiral-bound printout of the original documents in her lap. There were no ancient smells or crumbling parchment, just pages. The red facsimile booklet had arrived weeks before, accompanied by a typed note clipped to the front: "Translated from French. Estimated date: 1642. Source material: private collection, Zachary Levi, London."

Dijon, France

My name is Countess Madeleine du Beaune. I am a French Aristocrat, born into a wealthy bourgeois family. I grew up in a giant stone manor in Dijon. Like all family members, I was well educated, even in the arts and sciences, which was untraditional and not typical for women in my day.

I married Stéphane, a Count by primogeniture, whom I loved immeasurably. I married above my social status as he came from a lengthy line of nobles and was about to be appointed Duke by the King. My beauty, family, and wealth compensated for my lack of title. Indeed, I had all the refineries necessary for nobility. We married when I was 22, and he died six years later from a black fever that swept France in the spring.

Although custom forbade it, the King, knowing my husband's wishes that the estate be mine, made an exception and issued a rare royal decree granting temporary estate stewardship to his widow, Madeleine. He left me the Beaune estate, including the chateau, the tapestries, lavish furnishings, vineyards, and the gold Stéphane never cared for.

My Domain is vast and envied by many. I have always favored charitable works; yet my life became entangled with the aristocracy and the management of the land.

God did not bless us with children, so after Stéphane's death, his younger brother Étienne assumed the title of Count. He urged me to simplify my life and allow him to manage the estate. My good brother-in-law understood how opportunistic cads prey upon widows with wealth, so he gladly tended the land and the peasants, while I retained ownership.

I could not leave the place where my memories of Stéphane were so happy and where he lies at rest. I receded from public view. I candidly admit that I became a lonely widow.

I believed I was protected. Instead, I was exposed. The nobles were outraged that a woman should hold land of such scale, even temporarily. They called it unnatural. Soon they began to whisper that I had tricked the King, that the decree was forged, that I had no rightful claim to the estate. The rumors festered like rot in the vineyards. They said I bewitched the court.

I have waited until this moment to put pen to paper, though the memories have never left me. Now that I am safe, I find the words rushing back with a force I cannot contain. I do not write to clear my name. I write because I survived, and because what they did to me was cruel and calculated. Someday, people will understand Countess Madeleine du Beaune and learn from my tale. My story may help someone else in their darkest and loneliest hours. Let the record live where justice failed.

The Arrest

The storm had been coming for weeks. A leaden sky had hung low all week, but the heavens released a torrent of water that morning, and ill-tempered rain pounded against my windows. I stood there, watching the assault, hoping for a reprieve. Soon, however, it was impossible to see even a stone's throw away as the heavy fog rolled off the sea and snaked its way through the streets.

I felt the heaviness in the air and realized that my perception of what was happening around me was obscured. Now, I thought of the glances of my servants and the sudden absence of friends who once filled my drawing room with laughter. I dismissed it as the sorrow of widowhood and other people's discomfort with being around a grieving woman.

My ominous hunches began a while ago with the silence of my trusted, amicable maid Élodie, who had been with me for years. She grew stiff and cold; lately, she had shrunk from me as if I were contagious. She disobeyed me, even arguing about lighting lamps to cheer the household, claiming oil was scarce for the impoverished peasants working on the property. But behind her defiance was something more profound. I tried to get her to warm up to me, reminding her of who we once were to each other. But having heard rumors, Élodie had already judged me.

I admit I changed during the many months of stress in my household. My appetite waned, and I began to lose weight. My monthly flow ceased. My skin was no longer as supple, my moods shifted more quickly, I tired easily, and my energy was uneven. I lost interest in things that once thrilled me. But I knew then, as I know now, that I am sane. I know my name and purpose. And I know the difference between womanhood and wickedness, between erudition and the dangers of ignorance.

The day of the arrest came cloaked in dreary fog. I stood at the hearth, wistfully, remembering better days. A strange foreboding nagged me as if something unpleasant was approaching. Intuition was correct; late that night, I heard boots on stone stairs and men shouting. Strangers yelled out my name. Several men with grimy hands and sour breath burst into my room. I had been fast asleep. One man struck me before I could speak.

I shouted that I was the Countess, that they had no right to touch me. They laughed. "Are you Madeleine du Beaune?"

"Yes," I answered. And with that, I was no longer a court woman, but a sorceress.

It was then that the Police Chief, Claude Vasser, walked into my bedroom. The most powerful city official in the district had just watched his officer abuse me and did nothing to stop him. The officer quickly stepped to the side as Vasser approached, but not before he reached out and sent a warning cuff to my uplifted chin. I widened my eyes in fury and then focused on the officer.

Vasser's official badge stood out on his rain-drenched coat. As the Police Chief, he was the senior law authority. I knew I should have watched my tongue and been respectful. I had heard of his extreme cruelty; however, I was upset enough not to care about being irreverent, even as he moved towards me, holding an official-looking document in his hand.

Although Vasser thrust a document at me that I tried to look at, I noticed his gnarly rheumatoid fingers. At once, I felt compassion and outrage.

"You are under arrest, Countess," he said, dropping the paper. In the dim light of my bedroom, his sallow eyes bore into mine. I was dizzy with dread and fear.

"All of your dark activities must cease!" His voice was imploring and weary, as if he had been searching for me his whole life.

Dark activities? The shock of the accusation and the burning sensation on my wounds was incredible. Surely, he must have known I was not practicing a dark cultic activity! Did he not understand who I was?

"*Monsieur*, by what officialdom do you charge me?" I stood erect, and my eyes were level with his. I did not blink. I hoped my tone was threatening, that my stare intimidated him.

Immediately, I realized my mistake. Vasser was unaccustomed to having his authority challenged. His ruddy face twisted and contorted with rage. "By my authority, Countess," he growled and pointed at me, "And by my design, you are apprehended."

I shook my head in disbelief. Apprehended? Me?

I was neither a peasant nor a Parisian rabble-rouser to be pushed around. I was innocent of any crime, and to treat me otherwise was appalling! I decided to bring legal action against him and his officer. He would see; I would use my prominence to remove him from his position in government. He would not get away with such a misguided insult.

"You are in error, *Monsieur*," I retorted, too angry now to be afraid of him. "My lineage is of the bourgeois, and my husband's is of the nobles. I have always lived in France as an Aristocrat, and this is the city of my ancestry! No one has done more for Beaune and Dijon of Provence."

"You," he interrupted, stepping so close that I felt the steam rise off his wet wool jacket and fill my nostrils. "You have gone about to destroy this city and all the women in it with your evil practices!"

"This is a lie," I shot back through clenched teeth. "My husband's legacy is a testimony to who I am, and I have only carried out his wishes since his death. Remember that he was in the King's service as a royal officer. He was born into the noble families of Beaune and Lyon! He proved nobility in the 13th century and carried the Court Honors. His Highness, our Lord and King, was to promote and appoint him, Duke. I rode in royal carriages alongside him, and I will not stand for this nonsense!"

They dragged me from my chamber, past the sleeping guards, past Élodie, who did not come. I was alone. Of my 27 household servants, not one had appeared. Like a sack of grain, they threw me into the coach, no one caring that my wrists were bound behind me and that I could not break the fall. Tumbling onto the rough timbered floor, I barely had time to take a breath when a heavy boot kicked me from behind, hurling me to the back corner of the carriage.

Hannah rapidly turned the pages of the Countess's diary, riveted. She kept reading.

The Year in Prison

Eventually, I arrived at the Maison de Prison in Dijon, known to house the worst criminals in society and hailed as one of France's largest asylums for the criminally insane. It was legendary for its barbarity. The locals often referred to the place as the "Chamber of the Devil."

"This is a nightmare," I whispered, peering into the dark silhouette of the peeling walls and ceiling, smelling the foul miasma of human waste and decomposing lime and sand. I could hear the clandestine movement of rats, their sharp nails scraping the walls and floors nearby. From somewhere down the corridor, I heard screams.

Assuming my arrest was legal, my life was hanging in the balance. I was told that the official documents accusing me of practicing the Dark Art also listed the terrible penalty for those charged with such crimes. I began to grasp the limitations of my aristocratic standing in society regarding safeguarding my safety. Moreover, a widow without protection was most vulnerable to exploitation.

I was in pain and exhausted from knowing what lay ahead, the impossibility of reason in the face of ignorance. I thought about all those who became my enemies: friends, servants, the clerics and politicians, the conniving and ambitious nobility, and the so-called men of science. With their robed arrogance and small-minded prejudices, physicians backed by ecclesiastical power quoted false knowledge as sacred. They claimed that a woman past childbearing years, especially one unmarried and so outspoken, was inherently unstable, vulnerable to insanity, and susceptible to satanic possession. They argued that the body of such a woman, having lost its sacred purpose, became a vessel for evil because her soul was unguarded.

Before my incarceration, I had foolishly dared to write publicly that these assertions are not based on science, but on superstition. The absurd thing about the falsehoods is that they did not even apply to my circumstances. I was young enough to bear children. I lost my monthly flow because of my frailty. Though weary from grief and loss, my mind was still sound. And a woman's thoughts, insights, and care for others do not dry up with the womb.

My challenges infuriated everyone, prompting them to turn me into the target of a witch hunt. "Guard her, she may cause harm," they said. They labeled me as dangerous due to many other false beliefs and misunderstandings. It was a good excuse for the magistrate and politicians to seize my estate.

The men who claim to be healers have instead become jailers. They cite God and Galen alike, twisting words to trap us. What they fear is not illness, it is freedom; their inability to control a woman who knows her mind.

The Dark Night

Winter had ruled those months, but I stayed frozen even as spring crept into the world beyond these stone walls. My bones jutted through my skin. Starvation was not a punishment here; it was policy—two meals a day, which were scarcely edible. On Sundays, they provided only black bean soup. I counted the beans, one by one, until the bowl was empty.

The darkest night came just before my trial. I remember it not because of any dramatic event, but because it was empty, devoid of prayer and hope. I felt the full brunt of isolation. My belly ached from hunger. I remember the exact meal of tepid rabbit soup, barely warm enough to dull the ache, with a shard of bone I gnawed until it was white. I ate barley bread so hard it cut my gums, and still I swallowed every crumb. There was no shame left in me, only incredulous need and despair.

I had once been a woman of books, letters, and song. Through it all, I clung to fragments of sanity. I vividly recalled joyful memories of frolicking as a child; of my husband and I reciting tales aloud in the dark, including works by de La Fayette, Corneille, and du Bartas. My imagination and memories sustained me. I held out some hope that Étienne might intervene and save me.

I survived that year not because I was brave, but because I refused to die forgotten. This page will be available even if no one speaks my name after I am gone. I am Madeleine du Beaune. I was a healer, not a witch.

Chapter 21: The Witch Trial

Hannah continued to read the Countess's diary.

Dijon, France, 1642

Today will be my last day in this world. Of this I am certain. I stand on aching feet, wrists raw from ropes, in a courtroom packed with people not for justice, but for spectacle. A widow on trial for witchcraft is a delicious thing in France.

My body trembles. The cold cuts through my bones, but I force myself not to sway, not to plead. I have prayed and waited for Étienne, but he has not come. Perhaps he never received my letters. Or, like the rest, he chooses not to remember the vow he once made at my husband's grave, that he would come if I needed him.

The ride to the courtroom from the prison was brief. I reeled as daylight stabbed at my eyes. My head throbbed as I squinted into the morning. Everything was unbearable in its beauty. I wept without shame. At the foot of the courtroom steps, we halted. Officers conversed in hushed tones. I heard my name. For once, I dared not speak.

The courtroom brimmed with noise and disdain. Above me, guards argued about whether I deserved the screws or quartering. "Even Galileo would confess," one scoffed, "when joints are torn from sockets." Others joked about witches as "broom-riders," corrupted by

Satan. "A woman deceives because she was formed from Adam's rib, and everyone knows that Adam's rib was crooked!"

Mockery abounded. A man shouted from the balcony, asking where my jewels were. "Have you forgotten how to dress as a noblewoman?" Another woman declared I looked like a fisherman's wife—not one whose husband brings fish home. The woman tightened her coif. "We should all thank the Blessed Mother that Countess du Beaune does not have on her jewels! That Venetian ring of hers might have been the death of us! Who knows what innocent woman would have been harmed today if she could dispense her poisonous vengeance?" She folded her arms. "*Humph,* I know her kind."

The crowd's temperament instantly darkened. The mention of poison took the bloodthirstiness and feigned lightheartedness out of the moment. This scandalmonger gave these people one more reason to condemn me. In truth, I have never owned a talisman nor ascribed lucky charms with mystical powers. I most certainly have never possessed poison.

I tried not to let my lower lip tremble. Still, I did not cry. I whispered Étienne's name like a prayer. I was alone, condemned before I could speak.

Then, the courtroom theatrics intensified. A court clerk flounced in wearing scarlet and lace, squeaking out ceremonial announcements with exaggerated flair. He was absurd, a caricature, like a jester, yet he heralded absolute terror: "This tribunal shall now judge Madame Madeleine du Beaune, under the reign of King Louis XIII."

"God save the King," they shouted. *But will God save me?* I wondered in silence.

Two jurors, Pierpont and Beaufort, entered with the prosecutor LaMotte. I recognized them all. They once dined at my home. They now nodded solemnly as if they had never seen me before. They instigated my imprisonment and condemnation because of their greed, to seize my estate and gain massive wealth. My fate was being decided by men who had drunk my wine, praised my hospitality, and who now would not look me in the eye.

The Judge burst into the room like a pent-up bull unleashed. Judge Louis Ambroise, swathed in black, his robes billowing, his mood thunderous. The spectators buzzed with anticipation, but he showed no regard for their excitement. He glared at his stack of papers, scowling at them as if they had personally offended him. He ignored the clerk's fluttering antics. He ignored me.

Finally, he looked up and lifted his gavel. With a bang, he silenced the crowd. "Quiet in my courtroom," he bellowed, his jowls drooping low against his neck, hanging like the dark puffs of bags under his eyes. His eyes settled on me. He peered through horn-rimmed spectacles, *pince-nez,* his expression shifting from cold disinterest to open contempt. I felt myself naked, undressed by his frank stare, stripped of dignity.

Thus began my trial, one of the most anticipated ever to be heard by this court. Then came the accusations.

The clerk stood and read the charges aloud: consorting with the devil, spreading pestilence, corrupting the faithful, violating the laws of modesty and nature. My breath caught on the last one. "Violating nature." That charge condemned every woman who dared to age, think, and live alone.

The witnesses paraded in. A midwife from Beaune claimed I had touched a stillborn child and smiled. A baker's daughter said I placed rosemary on a doorstep, and the next morning her father choked on his bread. A former lover's cousin insisted I cast a spell to "steal his virility." Each lie, more absurd than the last, drew murmurs of delight from the gallery.

They saved their most condemning witness for last. They called Mademoiselle Danvers. I nearly collapsed upon hearing her name.

She had been my bath maid that winter before my arrest; a simple, illiterate, fearful girl, unable to form a complete sentence. How could she testify? The prosecutor, Anton LaMotte, had undoubtedly fed her lines until she could stammer them back on cue.

I watched from my seat as LaMotte grinned, shaking his finger at me like a villain from a pantomime. The crowd leaned in, enraptured. The prosecutor adjusted his powdered wig, took center stage, and thus began the spectacle.

"Mademoiselle Danvers," he boomed, "do you recognize the woman standing accused of satanic arts and witchcraft?" She did not reply.

He mocked her by asking if she was deaf and if she intended to waste the court's time. She trembled and giggled nervously. Her silence made her more compelling, not less. The room was rapt.

When he pounded the jurors' table, she flinched so hard the entire chamber froze. Then the absurdity began.

"Yes," she finally said, "I saw the Madame dancing."

The prosecutor gasped. "Dancing? With whom?"

"With the fairies," she whispered.

The room erupted. Men shouted. Women crossed themselves. The Judge pounded his gavel to no avail.

She continued, her eyes wide with terror, speaking of herbs, Devil's Claw root, and Witch Hazel. "She made brews," the girl said. "Salves with ashes of toads for her spells."

I had once told her I felt "hotter than the Devil's baby." It had been a joke, a turn of phrase. But now she repeated it, convinced it was an omen of evil. My words, stripped of context, became damning proof.

The prosecutor played the crowd. He repeated her testimony, twisting each phrase into poison. "A brew of Saint John's Wort! Devil's

Claw! Black roots for the black-hearted!" He turned to the jurors and proclaimed, "This is the concoction of Diablo's mistress!"

The girl cried, pleading for the court to believe her, swearing on her sister's grave. Then, the final blow:

"Did you see the demon's mark?" he asked.

"Yes," she said. "On her forehead. She said she was red hot."

"And what did you think she meant?" he pressed.

"She was laughing," the girl replied. "Gleeful, like she liked it."

I felt my blood boil. The crowd hissed. The jurors nodded. The Judge glared.

LaMotte, Pierpont, and Beaufort stood, and each gave impassioned speeches about women's inherent weakness. They quoted scripture. Eve's fall. The serpent. Again, Adam's rib was mentioned. They said my intellect made me dangerous, and my independence made me monstrous.

LaMotte's prosecutor dismissed Mademoiselle Danvers with a sneer, as if shooing away a fly. "You may step down now, Mademoiselle."

For hours, I endured the twisted, scandalous testimonies. Accusers told lies; the truth was unwelcome there. I remember when Beaune was plagued two decades ago, when death came quickly and hope slower still. That grief was sharp, but it was not cruelty refined.

They said I consorted with devils, that I poisoned infants. I survived the plague when others died because I made bargains in the dark. I could once remember every face I aided. Now, I saw them turn from me, friends, neighbors, and women whose children I once saved. They accused me of withering crops, deliberately causing a nobleman's wife to miscarry, whispering to birds, and poisoning the wells. All falsehoods, but enough to ignite and stoke the flames. That is how it works in the court. You do not need to be guilty. You must be an inconvenient nuisance, an iconoclast challenging convention and ignorance.

The trial dragged on until noon. Then the Judge's eyes lifted to look at the clock. His belly hungered more than his conscience. Burgundy wine, his *pot-au-feu* stew, and a chunk of round Auvergne cheese were foremost on his mind.

The Judge asked if I had a statement. Every bone in my body was hurting. But I stood.

"I am Madeleine du Beaune." I said, "I have healed your children, tended the sick, and buried your dead."

"You were paid for your services?" LaMotte snapped.

"I accepted only thanks. I neither needed nor wanted material goods."

The Judge leaned forward. "Do you deny consorting with dark forces?"

"I deny nothing that is not true," I answered. "And I affirm nothing you put in my mouth. I have done nothing wrong."

There was a brief, electric pause. Then came cruel jeering and laughter.

He banged his gavel. "Order!" But the order had already been decided.

Finally, the moment came. The clerk reappeared, dramatically announcing that the court would deliver its verdict.

The Judge declared, "Countess Madeleine du Beaune, you have been found guilty of practicing witchcraft. It is plain to me that you have ignored the most widely respected writings and warnings."

There was no gasp of surprise. The trial attendees expected the verdict. Judge Ambroise picked up the *Malleus Maleficarum*, the hideous handbook of Inquisitors, and quoted it as if it were holy writ: *"All wickedness is but little to the wickedness of a woman. What else is she but unavoidable? A desirable calamity? Women are by nature instruments of Satan; a structural defect rooted in creation."*

The courtroom erupted. Men shouted. A woman screamed, "Plague spreader!" as if I, and not their negligence, carried death into homes.

The Judge's gavel slammed again. "You are condemned, Madeleine du Beaune. Tomorrow at dawn, you will die by burning. You will be taken to the cell at Chappel Saint Lazare for last rites and Final prayers."

My legs nearly gave out. The world tilted. All hope was lost. My mouth stayed shut. Not because I was brave, but because screaming was useless. They do not listen to screams. They only hear confession.

The room emptied quickly, and in a panicked rush to get me out of the building, I was pulled, pushed, and shoved, a needless demonstration by those in charge. I stood on the back of a horse-drawn wagon with my hands tied. They took me to St. Lazare.

I was stunned at the smell hovering in the air as we descended the last hill before we arrive at the chapel, where they throw me into a cell. The stench is of burnt hair and flesh, a smoky, foul smell that shakes me. It is the odor of a reality that is raw and savage, of a horrifying death waiting for me around the corner. From what I could see as we passed by the square, there were the bodies of small people, whose trials preceded mine. I started to panic. They did not intend to hang me. Fire is cleaner, they said. Fire is biblical. I believe I fainted.

Hannah read avidly. She was familiar with the *Malleus Maleficarum,* Latin for "The Hammer of Witches," written in 1486 by Heinrich Kramer and Jacob Sprenger. It is one of the first things that comes up when searching online for 17th-century European witchcraft.

The book was hugely popular, as it was the Bible of medieval treatises on witches. It instructs magistrates on how to identify, interrogate, and convict witches.

Hannah wondered if there is any hope for Madeleine at this point. The accusations, the scapegoating, and the finger-pointing at Madeleine unsettled her. She was jarred by the idea that all people are prone to stereotypical thinking. It vaguely reminded her of how she treated her mother, condemning Addie for her flighty ideas and her spiritual pursuits. In a way, she now felt no better than these people in the court, getting ready to destroy Madeleine.

Hannah's mind wandered to accounts of the smell of burned flesh. Of crematoria, skeletons in mass graves, and the Holocaust. She remembered Dr. Jo's story about her trip to Varanasi, India. Hannah had chills from the eeriness of such thoughts, and her skin crawled from the associations. She was now sure she knew the smell of burnt human flesh. *Are humans like the mice whose offspring inherit an aversion to the odor of cherry blossoms?* she wondered, then tried to shake it all out of her mind and continued reading the diary.

March 3, 1642—Eve of execution
From the cell beneath the Chapel of St. Lazare

Étienne wore a friar's cassock and a velvet cap that masked half his face. He had received official clearance as a priest from the magistrate. He brought the guards bottles of wine and gold coins, claiming them a gift from a grateful nobleman with influence. My brother-in-law also got a sack of clothing for my burial, and a small prayer book. He encouraged both guards to join him in drinking. Thinking themselves invincible, they drank with abandon and fell asleep.

Étienne waited until the guards appeared stuporous and the sisters had gone to sleep after kneeling for their midnight rosaries. Then he came to me quietly. I was seated upon the cold bench, my hands folded in my lap, my hair unbound.

Étienne knelt before me and laid the sack at my feet. That was when I knew it was him. Overjoyed, I embraced him, thanked him for coming to rescue me, and asked him how he knew where I was and what had happened. He had overseen my situation while staging the escape with a few loyalists. They plotted a plan and determined who would accept bribes.

"It is a long story, not for now," he said. "There is little time," he whispered. "The firewood is already stacked. They will come for you before sunrise."

He reached into the sack and removed a noblewoman's mourning attire. There was a dark blue dress with an embroidered bodice, a high collar, and modest skirts. Beneath it, he had hidden a velvet cloak, a woman's riding gloves, and a pair of worn boots.

"You must dress quickly. The figure is prepared and will take your place."

"A corpse?" I asked him. "Or straw?"

"Both," he said. "A girl from the debtor's ward took her own life yesterday. They will not know, because her face is veiled. The wrists are bound. The blood they expect to see is painted upon her chemise. And none here wish to gaze too long upon a witch. The guards will carry her because they already know you are faint and too weak to walk."

His words struck like a bell beneath the ribs, but I said nothing. He poured a silver key into my palm.

"You will unlock the side grate when the moon is at its highest. I will wait with a mare. God willing, we shall be in the forest before the bell strikes seven."

I looked at him then, this man who had once loved my husband, who now risked all for me. His eyes were not soft. He did not ask for forgiveness. He placed his hands upon mine as if steadying a blade.

Why?" I asked him. "Why do this?"

"Because I believe in the truth and you do not belong to fire," he said. "And because I loved my brother. I love you, too. In God's name, they would wish it themselves."

He turned then and left the cell with his prayer book and the empty sack, humming a false litany. I nearly laughed aloud. The guards cheered his exit and asked if the Devil had left my body. He told them yes. They asked if he had seen him go. He said he had.

Now I sat dressed in borrowed silk, the dead girl curled in my pallet like a broken doll beneath a veil soaked in camphor. I prayed they would not look too closely. I prayed the wine was strong. I prayed the ropes would hold.

They would light the fire in the square at dawn, and the crowd would cheer when the flames find the hem of her skirt. Some would cross themselves. Others would spit. They would say they saw me flinch. They would say they smelled brimstone. They would say justice was served.

Let them, I thought, *I will be long gone by then.*

We fled, riding by night and resting by stream beds, taking new names at each village gate. We moved like stealthy thieves. As "Madame Delon" and "Étienne de Maruei," we made our way slowly toward Aix-en-Provence, where no one asked questions of weary travelers with coins and clean papers. In a chapel hemmed by olive trees, we were wed in a quiet ceremony by an old priest with poor eyesight. We remained in the south through the following summer, living modestly, savoring the safety of obscurity. There, I began to reconstruct my story.

Three years after the trial in Dijon, the danger had cooled, as we received word that the Police Chief, Claude Vasser, was dead. The prosecutor, La Motte, had also passed away. Once we were certain that the small amount of gossip circulating among the nobles and Vasser's henchmen no longer piqued curiosity, we returned to Beaune with our newborn son, whom we named Jacques. Our marriage certificate bore the names of Monsieur Étienne du Beaune and his bride, Geneviève Delon.

Officially, Madeleine had been executed and perished by fire at the stake, and Étienne, as the deceased Count's sole heir, had lawfully inherited the estate. The laborers and commoners never questioned my fate, nor did they consider that I was still alive, as it was unheard of for a witch to escape the fire. The families who worked the land restlessly in his absence, fearful of seizure or famine without noble oversight, welcomed Étienne's return. No one questioned the identity of his soft-spoken wife, my face half-veiled and my tinted auburn hair tucked beneath a velvet cap. No one recognized my robust figure as the woman whose name had darkened Dijon; it had been five years since I was forcibly removed from my home in Beaune and imprisoned. Étienne and I rarely spoke of those terrible times again, but I planted rosemary in a circle every spring and named each bush after the silenced women who did not escape.

Hannah set the pages down for a moment; She felt goosebumps and shivered. She contemplated all the people who, for millennia, had screamed. They screamed in courtrooms, in bedrooms, in darkened alleys, into pillows, and to the heavens. They cried out for mercy, safety, and dignity. But no one listened. Or worse, they heard and stood by idly.

Hannah thought of her editor talking to her about the assignment to uncover what "all the buzz was about" with Dr. Jo's concept of inherited emotion, and how she should not write fluff but something substantive. Dr. Jo, whom she revered, was brilliant, unapologetic, and dignified. Would she have been condemned as well for poisoning minds? For blasphemy? Addie, her woo-woo, witchy, new-age mom, once lit a sage candle and told Hannah that her soul had memories even if her mind did not. With an open mind, it no longer sounds ridiculous. What would have happened to her in 1642?

Hannah thought of her initial skepticism and judgmental attitude about the assignment—about trying to tell these stories, not just as a journalist but as a witness. This work of telling stories and updating the narrative as we moved along was a way to lift the echo of those screams and finally let them be heard and understood.

Hannah thought of Eli Wiesel, a Holocaust survivor, Nobel Laureate, and author, who said, "Anyone who listens to a witness becomes a witness." Bearing witness is not just the survivor's responsibility, but also that of those who listen to their story.

Hannah had an unexpected epiphany about her psyche, which hit her like a lightning bolt. Although lately she was gaining awareness of the origins of her mean behavior toward her mother, this was the first time she realized how intolerant she was, no better or different than the lowlifes in the courtroom trying to destroy Madeleine. For years, being with her mother provoked perennial eye rolls and sniggers, which Addie tolerated, considering her behavior a delayed adolescence feature of the Separation and Individuation process. In a different context, Hannah was overcome with sorrow, dismayed by her mother's temperament and outlook. She promised to change and acknowledge her mother for the wonderful, solid person who had always supported and raised her unfailingly and selflessly.

Hannah paused to ponder the page still open in her lap as she took a few deep breaths. Madeleine's words were so clear that it felt like she had just said them in the room.

Hannah had first imagined Countess Madeleine du Beaune as a seducer, even a manipulator; another woman shaped by legend. But now, she saw her in a different light. She had lived in a time when female agency was conflated with witchcraft, when healing herbs and dangerous truths were evidence of sorcery and spells punishable by death. The Countess was too wise, outspoken, ungoverned, and self-assured for the times in which she lived. And, like Maria, she had paid for it. Their stories were in sync.

Hannah imagined Maria, in Washington Heights, sewing by the window in a tiny apartment above Broadway, raising Ella with quiet ferocity. She imagined

Maria never dating again, carrying shame she never earned and grief she never spoke aloud. She thought of Ella, too: young, hopeful, violated, then silent and alone.

And herself. A daughter in the lengthy line of descendants.

She returned to the final page of the Countess's diary:

To the women who read this, you are not cursed, broken, or alone. They will try to silence you. But each time you speak out, you carry us forward.

Hannah closed the facsimile, letting the last page rest under her palm. The pages were thin and modern, but the voice that filled them was centuries deep. She did not require the original to feel its weight. The story had survived for millennia through fire, silence, and time. And now, it would continue through her.

She whispered to those who came before her, "I hear you."

Chapter 22: Wise Elders

Later that week, while Hannah was immersed in reading the Countess's diary, Graham arranged to visit Zach for a mid-morning cup of brew. Graham knew that Zach had invited Hannah to see him that same afternoon.

Zachary Levi moved with surprising agility for a man of 94. He had dressed that morning with deliberate care: new blue jeans, a dove-gray cashmere sweater, and worn, beloved loafers that carried the scuff marks of memory. He had a scholar's gaze that did not simply look at you, but through you, as though examining the architecture of the soul.

Graham sat across from Zach in the paneled library, absently swishing the tea in his cup with his teaspoon. The oak shelves, which were lined with books from the wainscoting to the ceiling, were a testament to Zach's scholarship. Graham noticed many rows of books dedicated to Jewish history, philosophy, art, and literature. Zach sensed that Graham was preoccupied.

"I've been thinking," Graham began, "about how to make this work with Hannah. Not just the logistics. The life. About how to honor something that isn't mine. I never gave much thought to faith before. But she feels Jewish so deeply. It's not so much about faith as it is existential. I see that now."

Zach raised an eyebrow. "I'm glad you see that. You've never struck me as a man afraid of commitment. It doesn't have anything to do with that?"

"It's not the commitment," Graham said. "It's wanting to do it well. I've spent many years listening to you talk about memory and belonging. About why it matters. And now it's all real. It's not an abstract concept anymore."

"Are you worried you'll get it wrong?" the old man asked.

"Some of that. And some of the things I absorbed as a kid. My parents weren't hateful. Just small-minded. The kind of people who called anything unfamiliar, 'exotic' or 'interesting' in that tone that meant they were afraid of it. I don't want that mental chatter around my own family. I love Hannah and want to marry her, and being Jewish is part of who she is."

Zach nodded. "I knew your father. I remember. That is the gift of grief, sometimes. It leaves you empty enough to fill with something better," he added solemnly. "Then you're already ahead of most people," Zach said gently. "You care enough and are conscious of what baggage you carry. You know, after ten years of working together, I can say you are an introspective, curious, and respectful man. You don't need to pretend you're something you're not. You just must keep learning."

Graham looked around the room. "You've taught me a lot already. About meaning making through stories. About survival. Why is none of it is as simple as religion on a census form? I am not thinking about converting," Graham went on, "But I want to understand what it means when our life together starts, when we have children, I want to be able to explain it to them. To show up and not sit there like a tourist watching a show."

Zach leaned back in his chair and agreed, "You need to know that Judaism is much more than a faith or religion. It's a culture of tradition, heritage, and memory. It's a story of survival, of helping others, and repairing the world. You learn by showing up. Light candles on Friday night. Tell your children where their people came from. Teach them our history, and not to be ashamed. It's the idea that the past belongs to you, whether you want it or not. You must decide what to do with it."

Graham exhaled. "So, there's no manual."

"No manual, but some wonderful interfaith classes are available," Zach said. "Mainly love, respect, and the willingness to keep trying keeps it real."

"I want Hannah to know I respect where she comes from," Graham said. "And I want our children to feel proud. Not confused, or having FOMO—Fear of Missing Out."

Zach smiled faintly. "So, you're planning children already!"

"Not this minute," Graham said, holding up a hand. "But eventually. Assuming she doesn't believe that I am a bigot or discover I'm completely unteachable and run for the hills."

"Oh, she'll discover you're unteachable," Zach said, deadpan. "But from the way she ogles you, she'll probably stay anyway."

Graham guffawed. "I'll take that as encouragement." Graham looked down at his hands. "I've always felt drawn to you because you have been like a loving father to me."

"And you, my boy, are like a son to me. Consider this conversation my blessing for you to marry my granddaughter," Zach said. "We don't give those out lightly."

"Thank you for your blessing. It means the world to me."

Zach's home was quiet when Hannah arrived. He invited her into his library, just as he had done with Graham several hours before. Zach had rummaged through books since Graham left that morning. A small tower of books was stacked on a table, appearing in danger of toppling. A framed page of Hebrew scripture hung near the window, which Hannah had not noticed before. Zach gestured for Hannah to sit beside him, not across from him, as if to say this was not an interrogation but an intimate conversation.

Hannah sat beside him on the old chenille sofa, warming her hands around a cup of her grandfather's favorite Fortnum and Mason's Royal Blend tea. The silence between them felt settled, like family.

"My dear Hannah, there are a few things I wanted to discuss with you so thank you for obliging me in coming today. Firstly, you know, I love Graham, and we are close. We have had a few important conversations lately." Zach went on. "He's been asking thoughtful questions about Judaism, about what it means to build a home that honors both of your histories."

"That sounds like him," she said quietly. "It's a tender topic and we've been treading lightly but need to face it."

"Perhaps you are treading lightly together; however, Graham is not approaching your relationship with Judaism lightly. He wants to understand it properly, not just to avoid mistakes, but because he wants to stand beside you without any pretense." Hannah felt taken aback, her fingers tightening around her cup of tea. She was flustered by the intrusion, a part of her feeling that her grandfather crossed a line.

"He loves you," Zach said gently. "Enough to look at the voices he grew up with and decide he doesn't want them shaping your life together. That takes integrity and character. And it's rare." She felt her grip loosen, surprised by her relief when she heard these words spoken aloud.

"He may not always find the perfect words," Zach continued, "But his heart is open. And so is his mind. You deserve that."

Hannah let out a slow breath, the tightness in her chest easing. "Thank you," she whispered. "I know, but it is good to hear from you."

"Now for the reason I asked you to visit me today; You know about Maria, but the plot thickens," Zach chirped.

Zach gestured to the side table, where a thick paperback rested under a folded pair of reading glasses. Its cover bore an engraving of a medieval scholar seated at a desk, quill in hand, eyes turned heavenward. Below was the title: *Portrait of a Seventeenth-Century Rabbi: The Life and Diary of Joel Nathan Levi.*

"I want you to have this," Zach said.

Hannah leaned forward, picking up the book carefully. "Who is he?"

"My ancestor, our relative." Zach said emphatically. "The Rabbi was a renowned Talmudic scholar and Kabbalist. He was a young man when he was appointed Chief Rabbi of Prague and Vienna in the early 1600s, where he found himself at the center of an anti-Jewish campaign orchestrated by the Hapsburg

Empire. During this time, the Emperor Ferdinand imposed excessive taxes on Jewish communities. Rabbi Levi was appointed to oversee a commission for assessing these taxes among the Jewish communities he served. Trying to be even-handed, the Rabbi and his committee devised a plan to collect the most from the wealthiest individuals, and the least from the poorest."

"Sounds fair," said Hannah.

"Yes, but…there was a large and wealthy Jewish community inhabiting an area near the main palace, called Leopoldstadt. It was already costly to live there. The Rabbi's attempt to increase taxes there backfired; his decision sparked widespread outrage among the rich merchants, who argued that imposing higher taxes on them was unfair. The good Rabbi agreed that it was unfair to them specifically, but it was a just, morally correct decision for the greater good of the Jews, under the circumstances. The Jewish merchants thought otherwise, of course. They perceived Rabbi Levi as dangerous, because he had a voice and a following. Today he would be called an influencer. So, the wealthy merchants denounced the Rabbi to the king, accusing him of publicly slandering Christianity. As a result, the Rabbi was imprisoned and sentenced to death by Ferdinand. However, many community members protested the sentence, which was finally commuted to enormous fines, which took him many years to pay off, and a 40-day imprisonment in Vienna. Thereafter, he was exiled. While living in Poland, the Rabbi wrote his memoirs, recounting his experiences in prison. And here they are."

Hannah flipped through the pages. Hebrew on one side, English on the other. The translation was clean but dense, featuring many citations and extensive commentary. She looked up. "You descend from him directly?"

Zach nodded. "On my father's side. It's not just a rumor. There's a well-documented genealogy. My grandfather used to recite passages from the diary from memory."

She touched the pages again. "What was the Rabbi like?"

"Complex and complicated," Zach said. "Brilliant, devout, and so very modern for his time. He believed in education and reason. He was both a mystic, a rationalist, and pious at once. He wanted to bring order to chaos. That's why they locked him up."

Hannah sat back, letting the weight of the book rest in her lap.

"I thought you should know," he said. "Your heritage, it's not only a legacy of suffering and survival. There is scholarship. There is resistance and dignity. There is courage and compassion. There is a great deal that can be learned from your ancestors."

She didn't speak right away. Her fingers traced the edge of the book. "I used to think I had no ancestry," she said. "No bloodline that mattered. Just fragments and closed doors."

"And now?" Zach asked curiously.

"I'm not sure yet. But I feel like someone cracked open a window, like air coming into a stifling room. I am so intrigued." She looked up at him and blithely said, "Tell me something you admire about this Rabbi."

Zach didn't hesitate. "He didn't judge people too harshly. Even the ones who turned on him. He believed judgment belonged to God and that knowledge meant to serve compassion."

Hannah swallowed. "That's a rare stance for those days. He sounds enlightened."

"The Rabbi was so ahead of his time," Zach declared. "He taught his children the importance of tolerance and love for all. He was so open-minded that one of his daughters, an iconoclast, married outside of the faith. This brings us to an essential and meaningful connection. You recall that the Countess Madeleine du Beaune and Étienne (her former brother-in-law, who saved her from being burned at the stake) eventually had a son whom she named Jacques. He married the Rabbi's daughter, Leah. They met when Leah was on a study excursion in France, a rare thing in those days for a maiden to travel, let alone to study! You can imagine how much Jacques and Leah had in common; each was the offspring of a persecuted and imprisoned parent who didn't remain silent about the injustices they faced."

"Although the Rabbi was tolerant, he was pleased that Jacques chose to convert to Judaism and accepted him fully," Zach explained. "The couple remained in France. They or their descendants commissioned the fabrication of the mahogany trunk, which survived the centuries. Maria left it with me in London when she moved to New York. She wanted to leave her story behind. Besides, it was a long trip for a heavy piece. And as you know, the apartments in Manhattan are not so accommodating."

Zach lifted his cup again. "You come from people who endured, Hannah. But also, people who wrote things down, made meaning of their stories, and passed them forward."

She looked at the book again, heavier now with context. "So, this isn't just history. It's an inheritance."

"Yes. And a responsibility."

Hannah's throat caught on something like awe. "Thank you."

Zach shook his head. "No need. I just wanted you to know where you come from before you decide where you're going."

Chapter 23: Have Faith

Zach was crafty when meddling with Hannah and Graham. He intended to help them confront the complexities of faith and religion.

The couple spent most of that evening cleaning the kitchen and putting away the remains of a late dinner neither had tasted. They had circled the same conversation since their tiff over Graham's "exotic" comment, waiting for the moment they would be together in the flesh and both be ready to speak aloud.

They finally sat down together; Hannah folded her hands on the table and looked across at Graham.

"I keep trying to find the right words," she began. "This has all happened so fast. Sometimes I wonder if we're making it up, pretending it's simpler than it is. But I have never known a love that felt this honest," she said. "I have never felt so completely myself."

Graham watched her steadily. "It's natural to question a whirlwind romance; yet I return to the same feeling every time I do, that nothing and no one has ever been this clear to me."

She took a careful breath. "I have spent most of my adult life thinking I had to protect myself. After David died, I kept one foot out the door. With you, I don't feel that. I feel like this is my real life."

"I know we haven't known each other very long," he said. "But I have never felt this certain. Sorry if I am repetitive. I am not confused, and I am not afraid. I know we'll work out the whole religion issue. I am in."

"What are you saying?" she asked softly, holding his gaze. Graham stood up, walked over to Hannah. As he dropped to one knee, he retrieved a small velvet box from his pants pocket and opened it, revealing a sparkly, cushion-cut diamond solitaire ring.

"That I want to spend my life with you," he replied. "That I want to marry you. Hannah, will you marry me?"

"Yes, yes!" she said as he slipped the ring onto her finger. She jumped into his open arms. Hannah felt her heart expand with relief and wonder. She did not care how quickly it looked to others. *We know what we have together,* she thought.

"There's something else I've been thinking about," Graham said. "Something that matters just as much to me."

Hannah did not look surprised. "Tell me."

"I did not grow up with religion," he said. "My parents were good people, but we never talked about faith. They had narrow ideas, and to be perfectly honest, they harbored antisemitic prejudices that they never examined. That truth is embarrassing, mortifying. I think of it as mindless xenophobia. After my parents died I had to start over and decide who I wanted to be without their voices in my head. After I began spending so much time with Zach, especially, and now with you, I can see why having that connection to the past matters. It gives you something steady. I can see it's not just about faith. It's about good values, respect for all people, and helping others. You and I share those fundamental values and live accordingly," he continued. "I don't need to believe in God or be religious to be a good person. I don't feel tied to any tradition myself, so our feelings are mutual; and our children must grow up knowing that history."

Her eyes filled, but she tried not to let the tears spill. "It means everything to hear you say that" she whispered.

"I love you," he said. "And I love the parts of you shaped by everything your family went through. Even if it were possible, I would never ask you to leave your family past behind."

"Graham, you know I am not a religious, observant, or practicing Jew," she said. "However, being Jewish is an integral part of who I am. I am thrilled that you understand it is about survival and memory. My family made it through everything they did, which is why I am here. Being Jewish also comes with a set of values that respects, questions, promotes decency, and helps others, with the belief that every person has worth. I need you to know that. I don't expect our children to observe every tradition, but I want them to know where they come from, to understand their history, and those values."

Graham nodded, his expression thoughtful and calm. He smiled and tilted his head slightly.

"There is one more thing," Graham added. "Speaking of children, we are not 25 anymore. I don't want to wait a long time to start trying. If it takes a year, it takes a year. But I would rather begin right away than to put it off."

"I have been thinking the same thing," Hannah said, feeling the last of her hesitation dissolve. "We know who we are. We are not guessing. If we want a family, we should start."

"Absolutely. And if we have children, I want them to be rooted in your story. I am OK with raising them Jewish. I want them to be proud. And I want to be proud too, not standing on the outside."

"You won't be on the outside if you don't choose to be," Hannah reassured him. "There are ways to learn, including interfaith education classes, and community events. Even just being open and willing can suffice."

Their mood had shifted from excitement and joy to dutiful, serious and mature. At that point, Graham said, "We don't have to solve the problems of the universe and our future in one night. We have plenty of time to talk the rest of our lives to figure it out. It's late. Let's get into bed and continue our celebration there." Graham took her by the hand, and they went right to bed.

Chapter 24: Family Ties

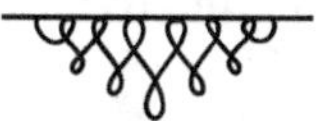

Zach invited Hannah and Graham to visit. A week had passed since their engagement, and he was thrilled to see them together. They sat in his library, excited to hear what Zach had to offer. His knowledge and wisdom dazzled Hannah, and more than that, she started loving her grandfather.

Zach admired the beautiful engagement ring that Graham gave Hannah when he proposed. The tea between them had cooled, but no one moved to freshen it. Something deeper than warmth was passing between them now, something like legacy. He tapped the edge of the scholarly Rabbi's biography resting on his lap. "You asked how to raise children who aren't confused," he said gently. "To pass something on without losing yourself. I think it is time you both hear the full story of Leah and Jacques."

Hannah and Graham both nodded in synchrony, their eyes steady on his. "You've heard pieces before," Zach continued, "But not the whole. And certainly not what they endured to be together." He paused, gathering memory while searching the table for some tissues.

"Hannah, you recall me telling you about the Rabbi, our ancestor. But Graham was not here that day, so let me recap. Rabbi Levi was a brilliant, disciplined scholar who served Jewish communities in Prague, Vienna, and later Kraków. He was revered but controversial, especially after he tried to institute a progressive policy: taxing the wealthier members of the community to ease the burdens on the poor. It cost him everything. The Rabbi was denounced by his congregation. Publicly humiliated, imperial authorities imprisoned him, and after his release, exiled him from Vienna altogether. His influence remained when he resettled in Kraków, but the trauma never left him."

Zach shifted slightly in his chair. "Indulge me in some repetition because you may already know some of the story. I promise this is important and relevant."

"Of course," Hannah and Graham murmured in unison. Zach continued.

"Leah was the Rabbi's youngest daughter. She was precocious, insightful, fluent in Hebrew, Yiddish, German, French, and Latin. She had a mind like his but a spirit all her own. After the Rabbi's imprisonment, the family sent Leah westward with relatives, partly for her safety, and partly for her to continue copying texts for a Jewish merchant family in Lyon. It was there she met Jacques."

Zach let the name settle between them for a moment. "Jacques du Beaune was not Jewish. He was the son of Countess Madeleine du Beaune, accused of witchcraft for refusing to relinquish her late husband's estate to envious nobles. You have read her story: torture, humiliation, escape. She lived with Étienne, her late husband's brother, who saved and married her. Jacques grew up beneath the shadow of that scandal. His mother lived in self-imposed exile from nobility. His father was a man who loved her enough to risk everything. Although the whispers stopped and memory seemed lost, Jacques knew what it meant to be judged before speaking a word."

Zach's voice quieted. "When Jacques met Leah, they didn't see enemies or anything foreign or exotic. They saw familiarity, drawing innumerable parallels between their parents' lives—being misunderstood, accused, persecuted, and imprisoned. He asked her a question about the destruction of the Temple, expecting a theological answer. Leah told him, 'When you carry memory, you protect what's still alive.' That was her way. She wasn't poetic, but a deep thinker who understood the importance of emotion in guiding our actions." Hannah motioned to her grandfather to hand her the book on his lap.

"Jacques fell in love with Leah's clarity, her loyalty to tradition. He loved her capacity to question. And she saw in him a kind of moral courage: an outsider who didn't try to charm or posture, but who listened. The Rabbi, for all his brilliance, had reason to be wary. His community had betrayed him. His daughter's heart was not a matter he took lightly."

Zach sipped some water. "But Jacques didn't run. He read. He studied Jewish texts. He asked the challenging questions. He never pretended to be something he wasn't. And after two years, he came to the Rabbi, not with a plea for permission, but with a declaration: 'I want to carry this with Leah. I was not born into it, but I've chosen Judaism.'"

Hannah looked at her grandfather with something like wonder. "And the Rabbi accepted him?"

"He did. But not immediately. First, he asked Jacques one question. 'What will you teach your children about our people?' And Jacques answered, 'That they came from pain and beauty, and that it is their task to hold both with reverence.'" Zach let that line land before continuing.

"That answer changed everything. The Rabbi knew that heritage is not just about blood. It's about carrying memory with tenderness. About honoring what you did not build but have inherited. That is what conversion meant to Jacques: not abandonment of his past, but full embrace of a future grounded in truth."

Hannah closed her eyes for a moment, then opened them. "I think Graham and I are both afraid of raising children who won't know where they belong."

Zach leaned forward. "Then raise them to ask where they come from. Raise them to love the question. That's belonging." He paused again. "But there is one more story. One the Rabbi himself often told stories in his later years. One that shook and shaped him more than other trials and tribulations." Hannah turned toward him, the air between them charged with suspense.

"Years after settling in Kraków, the Rabbi observed a man in his community. He was wealthy, quiet, and removed. The man was never seen giving to people experiencing poverty. With his deep sense of justice, the Rabbi gave a sermon condemning the sin of hoarding wealth while neighbors starved. He didn't name the man, but it didn't matter. The community understood. The man became an outcast. When he died, they buried him outside the cemetery wall."

Soon after, the orphanage lost funding, Sabbath meals stopped, and widows received no candles. Then came the truth. That man had been the anonymous donor behind nearly every act of charity in the community. He had given silently, never asking for thanks, and the Rabbi had misjudged him."

Zach's voice was gentle but unwavering. "The Rabbi was devastated. He confessed his mistake publicly. He said, 'I judged what I could not see. I failed to know what I did not ask.' And when his time came, he asked to be buried next to the man he had wronged, outside the cemetery wall. Not out of punishment, but as an act of repentance."

Hannah felt tears swelling, her nose congesting. She took Graham's hand.

"He knew he didn't fully know himself," Zach said. "He understood that even the wisest among us have blind spots. Our unconscious fears, shame, and our need to be right can all mask themselves as truth. And if we don't learn to examine our hearts, we will project our pain onto others. We'll judge too fast. Love is too late. Blame without understanding."

Zach turned toward them fully. "Hannah, from your brief description of your article about Dr. Brightman, I remember it highlights that we must know ourselves before loving anyone else. We will carry our pain like a mirror without self-examination, forcing everyone to reflect it."

Graham sighed deeply, nodding vigorously. "You are so right, that's exactly right."

"Yes," Hannah agreed. "That's exactly it. And I'm happy to report that I submitted it just before leaving New York. It has been accepted and will be published in a few months!"

"Wonderful!" said Zach. "Now, both of you, remember the story of Jacques and Leah," Zach said. "Remember the Rabbi and the man he wrongly condemned. When you worry about raising children in a mixed household, don't worry that they will be confused; ask yourself how to keep them curious. Teach them to question, honor, and know their stories."

Graham nodded slowly. He recognized and was deeply moved that this oratorio was principally for his benefit.

"Because memory," Zach added, "isn't just something we inherit. It's something we choose to carry. And when we do, we keep the story alive."

Chapter 25: Succession

Three weeks later, Hannah and Graham were married at a London courthouse in the late afternoon without a ceremony. Addie and Nate would not miss the marriage, despite Hannah minimizing the importance of the trip since they were not having a wedding party. But Hannah was especially thrilled that her mother was there. They spent the morning of the wedding together primping and telling stories.

Hannah's attitude toward Addie shifted entirely; she loved being with her mother and was grateful that she had come to London. Hannah apologized to Addie for lashing out at her abusively over the years. Her mother said, "All is forgiven. Now enjoy the moment and be the most beautiful bride!"

Zach arrived, leaning lightly on his cane. His expression was full of quiet pride as he kissed Hannah's cheek and clasped Graham's shoulder. They had insisted he come. Zach was family, the one who introduced them, the keeper of stories, the steady presence they both trusted, the one who deserved to see his granddaughter be well loved and love Graham in return. Zach was beside them, his eyes glinting like hers. He smiled with the warmth Hannah would carry with her.

They exchanged their vows and simple gold bands and then kissed as the people they loved watched with gentle, knowing smiles.

They had chosen each other with clear minds and open eyes and hearts, and that was enough.

A few months had passed since their wedding day. One ordinary morning, Hannah learned she was pregnant. She stood in the bathroom with the test in her hand, feeling extraordinary steadiness and gratitude for the luck and ease with which she had conceived. When she told Graham, he kissed her face and held her close, and neither tried to hide their tears.

They had just returned from the obstetrician: at 12 weeks, there was an audible heartbeat, and a small, solid shape appeared on the ultrasound monitor. Everything was excellent. Graham and Hannah cried quietly in the elevator while arm-in-arm.

Back at their flat in Islington, Hannah stood by the window, one hand resting lightly on her belly. She was almost 36 years old, and hers was considered a high-risk "geriatric pregnancy." And still, the baby looked good. She thought about how quickly life had passed her by. *Live and learn.* Hannah had never imagined that at 35, she would be married to the love of her life, thrilled about being pregnant and having a baby with Graham. The child felt like a promise, a connection that would continue forward. A living connection to a future built from everything that had come before.

Initially, Hannah had decided she wanted the baby's sex to be a surprise. She didn't want to be overly invested in having a boy or a girl and risk being disappointed if she became invested in one outcome or another. However, she forgot to tell the ultrasound technician this detail, who in turn failed to ask her if they wanted to know and exclaimed, "It's a baby girl."

The first drizzle of spring clung to the windows. The typical slow English weather made them feel more reflective and pensive. Graham sat back on his heels, helping Hannah unpack the last of her boxes from New York.

Now that she was safely through her first trimester, it was time to let a few people in on their news.

Hannah quickly emailed Dr. Jo:

I hope you're doing well. I want you to know I am married to Graham, the grounded and kind man I mentioned when we last met. And I am pregnant and thrilled. We live in London together. Also, as you must know by now, a funny thing happened: the article went viral online, and in print. It's strange seeing my own words quoted back to me. Thank you for helping me find them.

With love and gratitude,

Hannah Glass Pauly

Graham and Hannah called Zach next to announce the news. He was ecstatic, for them, and assured them he would be "hanging around" to meet his great-grandchild. Which he did.

Next, Hannah called her best friend Lucy, who despite the insanely early hour, shrieked in her usual hilarious comedic fashion and instantly demanded a belly photo, even though there was nothing much to see.

Hannah then scrolled down to Addie and Nate. She hesitated, not out of fear but from the gravity of it all. Hannah was surprised at how much she missed her mother. As she prepared to call her, Hannah thought of the women who had shaped her. What was borrowed, and what was broken? What had been handed down as law, and what could she rewrite as a choice? She thought of women who came before her—women in line. Good women were raised to be polite, to protect male egos, and to second-guess their discomfort. They had lived in eras where men were entitled, and women were punished for saying no, or worse, for saying yes. And their cries were ignored.

Hannah's ancestors, both men and women, carried memories. They told and penned stories. They spoke the truth when it mattered. They protected what they could and tried to love in their own way. Zach and Rabbi Levi. The Countess and Celeste. Maria and Ella. Gran and Addie. They had handed her pieces of their story. A lineage not just of blood but of meaning that informed and enriched her life's narrative in immeasurable ways.

She tapped the call button on the FaceTime application on her iPhone and turned on the camera. Addie was asleep in bed, but she answered on the second ring. They each turned on their video camera.

"Sweetheart. Hi…it's…are you OK, Hannah?" Addie's voice was warm and expectant. Her body language was clear, even with sleep in her eyes. "Is everything OK?"

Hannah smiled. Mom, "I am more than OK, I am great. We are both great. I have news that couldn't wait. I'm pregnant! Mom, I'm pregnant! It looks like we're having a girl!"

There was a pause. In concert, Hannah and Addie burst into tears. "You will be a wonderful grandma, as you are a terrific mother. You are the only mother who matters to me." Hannah said gently.

"I'm—I saw the signs—still…" She nudged her husband, still asleep next to her. "Nate, wake up, it's Hannah!"

"Addie, what's wrong? Hannah, what—"

"Dad! I'm going to have a baby! A girl!"

Betraying his machismo reputation, Nate too burst into tears. "I could not be happier. I love you so much, sweetheart."

"I love you too, Mom, Dad! And as you might know by now, my article for *Currents* is in print, and it has gone viral online!"

"We heard! We are so proud of you, Hannah," said Addie. "We can't wait to see you and Graham and the baby."

⁂

Addie came to London when Hannah was in her ninth month. Hannah and Graham had a beautiful, healthy baby girl they named Zelda, an amalgam of Zach, Ella, and Adelaide; a befitting honor to loved ones who had done their best. Addie stayed in London for a month to support the new parents.

Zelda thrived. Hannah lost her nervous edge. She was no longer a frightened woman with unnamed free-floating anxiety, running from meaningful relationships. Hannah, now the inheritor of many family stories and a legacy of connections, was evolving into a happy wife, mother, daughter, and stay-at-home freelance journalist with her own mental health column at *Currents*.

On a summer's day, Hannah and Addie strolled along Hampstead Heath, with Zelda in a baby wrap, tucked in and cozily asleep on Hannah's chest. Hannah knew she would be passing along some of the moments of angst to her beloved baby girl. But she would do what she could to protect Zelda from life's harshness. She would teach her daughter that tolerance and love begin with human connection, affection, and understanding of one's mind and family history. Hannah hoped to teach Zelda that inner strength and resilience come from knowing herself and creating her ever-changing life narrative.

Zach lived another year, enough time to fall madly in love with his great-granddaughter. During their last family visit with him, he told Hannah, "I am 95 years old and have lived a long, long life. I loved your grandmother, Maria, and I love you and little Zelda. I always will. You and my boy, Graham, found each other. Now, you know who you are. I am tired and ready to close my eyes."

That evening, Zach died peacefully at home with his family by his side.

Glossary of Terms

AMC (Automatic Mental Construct): Involuntary filters shaped by experience that influence perception. AMC is a term coined by the author of the non-fiction book *Yesterday Never Rests*.

Amygdala: A brain structure crucial for emotional processing, especially fear and memory formation under trauma.

Attachment Styles: Patterns of bonding shaped in childhood that affect adult relationships (secure, anxious, avoidant, disorganized).

Attachment Theory: Explains how early caregiver-child bonds shape a person's lifelong relational patterns and ability for emotional regulation.

Compromise Formation: Freudian term referring to unconscious mental compromises between opposing internal drives. The concept is related to the AMC.

Cortisol Dysregulation: Abnormal patterns of cortisol release, often seen in trauma survivors, and contributes to chronic stress and anxiety.

Dissociation: A mental disconnection from the present, often due to trauma; can involve depersonalization or memory gaps.

Epigenetics: The study of how trauma and environment can affect gene expression across generations without altering the DNA sequence itself.

Hypervigilance: A state of increased alertness and sensitivity to threats, commonly resulting from trauma or PTSD.

Implicit Memory: Memory that is unconscious and non-verbal, often expressed through emotions and body sensations rather than recollection.

Kindertransport: The Pre-WWII rescue mission transporting Jewish children to the UK, which separated them from their parents indefinitely.

Legacy Responsiveness: Heightened sensitivity to stress or conflict inherited from ancestral trauma.

Mindfulness: Intentional awareness of the present moment without judgment, used to reduce reactivity.

Neuroplasticity: The brain's ability to adapt and reorganize in response to experience or injury.

Post-Memory: An experience amongst the descendants of traumatic collective or personal traumas of parents and ancestors where the child imagines a connection to the past that shapes the present.

Post-Traumatic Growth: Positive psychological change experienced because of the struggle with highly challenging life circumstances.

Post-Traumatic Stress Disorder: A psychiatric condition lasting more than one month that develops after a person witnesses or experiences a life-threatening event.

Reflective Functioning: The ability to understand mental states in oneself and others; key to emotional resilience.

Sensory Flashback: A sudden, involuntary re-experiencing of trauma-related sensations without full narrative memory.

Survivor Syndrome: Emotional numbing, guilt, or shame experienced by those who live through atrocities when others did not.

Transference: Projecting old relational patterns onto current figures.

Trauma Fragmentation: Traumatic experiences are stored as sensory and emotional fragments rather than coherent memories.

Trauma Memory: Non-linear, sensory, and emotional memory stored primarily in the implicit memory system rather than declarative (explicit) memory.

Trauma Telescoping: The compression or collapse of past and present emotional wounds, disrupting time perception and emotional clarity by blurring temporal boundaries.

Wiedergutmachung: German reparation program for Holocaust survivors, symbolizing complex postwar grief and restitution.

About Jacqueline Heller

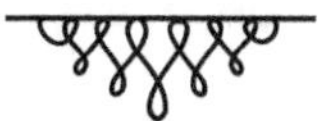

Dr. Jacqueline Heller, a retired board-certified physician and bestselling author, makes her debut as a novelist with *When Dreams Remember.* Her first book, *Yesterday Never Sleeps: Integrating Life's Current and Past Connections Improves Our Well-Being,* is in equal parts clinical, academic, and memoir, informed by her experience as a psychiatrist and as a child of two Holocaust survivors. She has contributed chapters and interviews to many publications, and is a frequent guest speaker on podcasts and syndicated radio broadcasts.

Over her nearly 40-year career, she maintained a private practice, volunteered at the Venice Family Clinic, taught and supervised psychiatrists in training and facilitated their process groups, led parenting groups, and introduced an Attachment Theory-based program to private schools.

Dr. Heller's interests include reading, Tai Chi, Scrabble, travel, tinkering (she holds three US patents), and spending time with her family. She and her husband live in Los Angeles, CA.

Acknowledgments

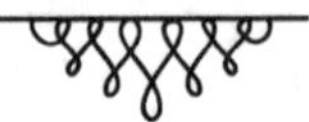

I owe a debt of gratitude to the following, without whom this book would not exist:

My husband, Gabe, for his unwavering support and tireless encouragement.

My readers, who offered valuable critical feedback: Elizabeth Brown, Naomi Schacter, Stephanie Laff, Judy Baumel-Schwartz, Jonathan Price, and Arlene Richards.

My editors, Carol Skolnick and Phyllis Stern, for tidying up the pages and catching things I missed.

You, the reader, for taking the time to go on this novel journey with me.

And of course to IPBooks, for giving me the opportunity to publish, making my dream become a reality.